TRACE OF HUMANITY

JULIET CARDIN

This is a work of fiction. Names, characters, places, and incidents are products of the author's imagination or are used fictitiously and are not to be construed as real. Any resemblance to actual events, locations, organizations, or persons, living or dead, is entirely coincidental.

World Castle Publishing, LLC
Pensacola, Florida
Copyright © Juliet Cardin 2023
Hardback ISBN: 9798392001590
Paperback ISBN: 9781960076588
eBook ISBN: 9781960076595
First Edition World Castle Publishing, LLC, May 8, 2023
http://www.worldcastlepublishing.com
Licensing Notes
Cover: Karen Fuller
Editor: Karen Fuller

CHAPTER 1

The sun shone through the window of the sixth floor, glinting off the CD in Bane's hand. He reflected the light against the wall, and Markley saw a shimmering, dancing orb that he began to stalk. The sleek black cat crouched low on his haunches, tail swishing back and forth, then he sprung like a panther, leaping up, claws extended, intent on catching his prey.

"Holy shit, you should see this cat go," he said into the phone.

"Bane, did you hear what I said?" Josie asked.

"Yeah, I heard, baby. Steaks are marinating, wine's chilling and I already tossed a salad," he said. She was still pissed he hadn't made reservations, but that had been intentional on his part. He wasn't about to propose in a room full of people. What if she said no?

"I said I'd be a little late. Jenko called a last-minute meeting, so don't start barbequing 'til seven. I don't want a cold dinner."

"Sure, no problem. Now see, if I'd made a reservation, we'd have been late. It all worked out for the best."

"I suppose," Josie agreed.

"See you when you get home." He hung up the phone. From the pocket of his pants, he pulled out a ring box. Putting down the CD, he flipped up the box lid and removed the one-carat diamond ring. Catching it in the light, he shone the reflection against the wall and watched the cat go nuts again.

* * * *

Josie squirmed in her seat at work. Six others sat around the table, not including Jenko. He rambled on, and Josie noticed she wasn't the only one fidgeting. Behind her boss's balding head was a huge picture window looking out over downtown. Being twenty stories up, it provided a dazzling view. Not that she could see much of it since he blocked it with his bulk.

Under the conference table, she stretched out her legs and tried to wiggle her toes in her tight, spiked heels. Her ass was cramping up from sitting so long. Boring meetings were a part of the job, but being salaried meant she couldn't clock any overtime. Not that she was hurting for money. Bane's income combined with hers—now that he'd finally moved in—allowed them to lead a decent life.

"Spring line-up is huge," Jenko reminded them. "Last quarter left us flat, and we need to vamp things up if we want to stay on top."

He'd said the same thing this time last year. What did he expect when they designed beachwear? Winter had been mild, so no one was in a hurry to leave town for vacation. Plus, people just didn't have the money to take off somewhere warm at a moment's notice. Especially when the economy was still recovering.

Josie stifled a yawn and focused on the blue sky over Jenko's head. These meetings always made her mind wander. *God, my feet! Why does it always smell like burgers in here? I wonder if Bane fed Markley?* She tried to refocus and concentrate on her boss's words.

Half-past six, and the light was still good. The longer days were nice. No more going to work and coming home in the dark; talk about depressing. Now she could look forward to hanging out at the beach after work which was just a short ride from their apartment.

Tonight would be special. Two years was a long time for a relationship. A turning point. After two years, you'd know if you were gonna make it or fall flat. Josie hoped it was the former. Bane was the best thing that'd happened—

"What the hell is that?" Kevin demanded. He stood up and pointed over Jenko's head.

Josie's rumination broke as she stared with her co-workers out the window where Kevin pointed. Even Jenko turned around, though he wore a look of annoyance on his face. She barely became aware she was up on her feet and darting across the room like everyone else.

"Holy shit!" she gasped.

There in the sky, floating silently and effortlessly, was a giant circular object stretching over a hundred feet across, gray in color, with a black band around the center. The top half had a row of lights that shone outward through what appeared to be tiny windows. It hovered so close it seemed to be looking right into the office.

A freaking UFO! Just like in the movies. Josie didn't know how she felt—in shock, most likely. Its presence could be interpreted as many things: horrifying, intriguing, groundbreaking. After complete silence for almost a full minute, everyone started speculating at once.

"This is it. An invasion. My God!"

"We're screwed! Look at everyone down there. They're swarming like ants."

"They're freaking out. Shit! I'm freaking out."

"Calm down!" shouted Jenko, always the clear-headed, take-charge leader. "It's probably some kind of advertising stunt."

Though a couple of people nodded their heads, grasping at straws that he was right, Josie felt deep in her gut they were in trouble. That thing out there was no stunt. This was the real deal. They watched, transfixed, at the window.

"Nothing's happening," Tara said. "It's just sitting there…waiting."

"Waiting for what?" Brian asked.

"Damned if I know," Tara replied.

"Well, I'm not gonna wait to find out. I'm outta here," Kevin said. He rushed for the door, and everyone else followed except Jenko and Josie. As their co-workers pushed through the door in a frenzy and made a break for the elevator, Josie looked at her boss.

"What should we do?" she asked.

Jenko kept his eyes fixed on the object. "Don't panic. We should leave, but don't take the bloody elevator."

Everyone had gone by the time they got out into the main office. Josie snatched up her purse and jacket as they whizzed by her cubicle and strode quickly to keep up with Jenko. He headed for the doorway leading to the stairs, and they both squished through at the same time.

Twenty floors. Thank God we're going down, not up.

When they reached the lobby, Josie saw it wasn't quite deserted. About a dozen people stood at the huge window by the main double doors, staring upward. Outside on the street, she witnessed the mayhem. Some people stood stock-still, gaping up at the sky, while others charged down the sidewalks and weaved around, fleeing and stalled cars on both the road and the sidewalk. A few emergency vehicles drove by, dodging everything else while honking at pedestrians.

"We'll get flattened out there." She looked at her boss and noticed his hands were shaking as he took in the scene outside.

"Don't go outside," Jenko said, backing toward the wall. "Not safe."

Josie stared at him. Now was not the time to lose it. "I have to go out. I have to get home." *Bane must be freaking out.* She silently prayed he wasn't trying to get to her through this mess. No, he'd know she'd try to make it home. He'd wait. He *must* wait.

Jenko grabbed her arm as she turned to walk away. "Don't," he warned. "You'll die out there."

She broke free and moved back. "If you want to stay here, fine, stay. I'm leaving."

Before he could lunge at her, she darted toward the doors. As soon as she stepped outside, someone smashed into her. The woman muttered, "Sorry," and swung her small child up into her arms.

Josie watched her run down the sidewalk and disappear around the next street corner. Before Josie moved on, she tried to get her bearings. She couldn't catch a bus home like she usually did, not in this madness. It wasn't far to go, perhaps a fifteen-minute walk—or ten-minute run more likely. She kicked off her spikes and began to jog.

With the chaos all around her, she didn't make it to her building for almost twenty minutes. She'd glanced upward several times, keeping her eye on the UFO. It remained where it was, and thankfully no other ships had arrived—yet. She couldn't shake the foreboding in her belly.

She opted for the stairs over the elevator to her apartment. *Only six floors, not too much of a climb.* On the fourth floor, she stopped for a moment and caught her breath. *Please be home.* When she got to level six, she swung open the door and started down the hallway. Mrs. Jackson rushed past her, eyes glazed, and didn't spare her a word. The door to Josie's place was unlocked when she turned the handle. She went inside and shut and locked it behind her.

"Bane?" *You better be home.* In the living room, she saw Markley perched at the window, staring outside, his tail swishing back and forth. "Where's Daddy, baby?"

A noise down the hall got her attention. She practically ran down the hallway and flung open the bathroom door.

There, standing in front of the mirror, was Bane. She barely recognized him at first. He'd shaved his head. She caught sight of his eyes, watching her in the mirror. They were cold. When he turned around, she said, "Did you see…outside?"

"Yeah." He stared at her grimly and answered in a hard voice. "It's begun."

Bane was in shock—that must be it. Why else would he shave off all those dark curls she loved so much? Not that he looked bad. Just different.

Josie moved back against the wall as Bane stalked past her. He paused before the giant closet doors in the hallway and slid them open. Reaching up over his head, he pulled down a large duffle bag and tossed it onto the floor at Josie's feet.

"Pack only necessities. We travel light," he

said.

"What? Where are we going?"

"Somewhere safe. The city is compromised."

Josie stared at the bag. Bane pulled out his camping backpack—an on-going joke between them since he'd never camped—and strode past her into the bedroom. She picked up the duffle bag and followed him. He pulled open drawers and began tossing in clothes and items from atop the dresser.

"We can't just leave," she told him. "I have work tomorrow. And what about your book? And Markley?"

"You're not going to work tomorrow. Forget the book and the cat too." Bane marched over and picked her bag off the floor, and tossed it onto the bed. "Pack your shit, or I'll pack it for you."

Forget his book? "Why are you acting this way?" It was as if his entire personality had changed. The man standing before her was not the Bane she knew. She didn't want to know this man. Had the UFO affected him so badly? She knew fear did strange things to people.

Bane ignored her while pitching some of her clothes and toiletries into the duffle bag. He stuffed a blanket in as well and then picked up both bags and headed past her. Josie followed him and watched him rifle through the kitchen cupboards. He packed a frying pan, a small pot, and some cooking and eating utensils, along with a few sharp knives.

This was really happening. He was determined they were going to leave. Maybe she was the one with something wrong with her? Should she be taking this more seriously? Was it really an invasion?

She walked over to the window and stroked Markley's fur. The UFO still hovered in the sky. It was getting darker out, which made the thing appear even more sinister. It hadn't moved, and she didn't see any more of them. Perhaps it was friendly? Maybe just here for a visit?

She could see the army had arrived and was making its presence known. Helicopters darted around in the sky, though not too close to the spaceship. Military vehicles were all over the streets in addition to soldiers. This was some serious shit.

If Bane thought it best they leave, then fine, they'd leave. But damned if she was going to leave her cat behind. She headed for the closet but stopped when she stepped on something hard, hurting her foot. They were already sore and aching from the trip home, not to mention her nylons were practically shredded.

What the hell? It was a ring. An engagement ring, to be precise. She bent down and picked it up. She looked over at the kitchen and noticed the steaks marinating on the counter. Their second anniversary…had Bane planned on proposing to her tonight? She felt a lump in her throat. If it weren't for that damned UFO, she and Bane would be celebrating right now.

She slipped the ring into the pocket of her jacket and went to grab the cat carrier. Markley protested, but she managed to stuff him inside. Bane had taken his backpack into the washroom, and she saw him going through the medicine cabinet. He'd left the duffle bag on the kitchen floor, so she stashed a bag of cat food inside and Markley's food and water dishes. She also put her purse inside. Bane had already stuffed a few water bottles in the bag.

She set the cat carrier by the apartment door and hurried to change her clothes. Since they'd most likely have to walk—they didn't own a car, and maneuvering any vehicle outside seemed impossible anyway—she opted to put on a pair of thick socks, jeans, a t-shirt, a sweater, and her hiking boots. She was in the living room pulling on her jacket when Bane entered. He fastened up both bags and put them by the door. If he noticed the cat carrier, he didn't mention it.

"Ready?" he asked her.

"As I'll ever be. It's bad out there. I just came through it. Are you sure you want to go out? Maybe we should wait 'til morning?"

"No. The darkness will cover our escape. We leave now," he insisted.

"Our escape? Do you really think we're in danger? Couldn't it be friendly?"

"It's not."

Bane wrote sci-fi espionage for a living. He was good at it. But perhaps all that alien stuff had clouded his judgment? By the look on his face, she could see there'd be no reasoning with him. His mind was made up. And who knew, maybe he was right? They could be in danger, and leaving now might be their only chance.

Josie picked up the cat carrier while Bane swung on the backpack and picked up the duffle bag.

They headed out into the hallway, and she pulled the door shut and locked it behind them.

* * * *

Bane had seen the spaceship outside soon after hanging up the phone with Josie. It was Markley who first drew his attention to it. The cat had perched on the windowsill and hissed, tail swishing back and forth like crazy. Staring out the window, Bane had felt disbelief, then shock, followed by a sharp pain inside his head, which had made him drop to his knees. Images had flooded his brain, causing long-buried memories to rise to the surface. Memories that had no meaning in this world. It was as though they came from someplace else—some*one* else. But after a few minutes, everything had made perfect sense.

They were under attack. He knew that now. And he had a job to do.

Vaguely, he recalled who he'd been and the details of the life he'd led. He'd shaken off the lesser character while a stronger identity emerged—one hiding beneath the surface, awaiting its opportunity, its sole purpose. With lightning speed, he'd been reminded of his mission—his and several others who'd roamed the Earth with sleeping identities. Now they were united in their objective.

Survival.

* * * *

Bane slung the duffle bag over his shoulder as they left the building, leaving his hands free. He took Josie's hand in a tight grip, and they headed out.

Fear gripped Josie's belly, tying it in knots. Her eyes alternately scanned the spaceship and drifted among the people and their terrified faces. *Is this the end?* If she'd thought the chaos she'd raced through an hour ago had been bad, it was even worse now. The army's arrival had not curtailed the anarchy. In fact, it seemed to have enhanced it. Masses of people roamed the streets. Uniformed men and women tried to contain the mob and urged them to return to their homes. Everyone's heads were turned upward in anticipation and fear.

Bane seemed to have a destination in mind as he wound them determinedly through the streets. His steps were sure and quick, and Josie had to trust him. *Where are we going?* She wanted to ask him, but speaking was impossible. The frightened noise of the crowds and boom of megaphones firing instructions would drown out her voice.

The area beneath the spaceship was now cordoned off by fences and guarded by armed soldiers. Noticing the commotion, Bane drew up and headed down an alleyway, leading them on an alternate route. As they cut through another alley, a man suddenly lurched in front of them, holding a piece of rod iron. From inside his crate, Markley hissed. Bane stopped and pulled Josie behind him.

"Out of the way," Bane said. The cold tone of his voice sent a tremor through Josie. He didn't sound at all like the man she knew.

"End of the world," the man slurred, obviously drunk and deranged.

"For you, it will be if you don't move," threatened Bane. He gave Josie a nudge backward and shrugged off the duffle bag and backpack, his eyes never leaving his opponent.

The man raised the rod. As he brought it down, Bane grabbed it. A struggle ensued while Josie stood frozen in shock. "Stop it!" she cried. She put down Markley's crate in case she had to intercede.

Bane was a big guy, easily a foot taller than

Josie's five foot four. The man he struggled with was short but stocky. A glimpse of the attacker's face revealed sudden fear and exhaustion. He now clung to the rod in desperation, possibly wondering what would happen if he dared let go. She'd never seen Bane react with such violence before. He had always been the voice of reason and caution. Josie backed up until her rear end bounced against a pile of trash. All around, she could hear panicked voices and rushing footsteps. Strangely, the alley remained ignored.

Bane moved back enough to lift his booted foot and brace it against the attacker's belly. He shoved, sending the man reeling back to land on his ass on the pavement, dropping his weapon. Bane grabbed the rod and raised it up. Josie saw his intent as the drunken man cringed and lifted his hands.

"Don't! Bane, leave him be."

Bane shot a scowl at her before returning his attention to the drunk. "Get out of here," he snapped.

The man scrambled to his feet and fled. Bane released the rod, and it clattered to the ground. He pulled on the backpack and swung the duffle bag over his shoulder. Then he reached for Josie,

his expression cold. Quickly, Josie snatched up
Markley's crate. Hand in hand, they left the alley
and hurried down a dark street.

CHAPTER 2

Over an hour later, Josie and Bane were still walking. They kept to the far side of the jam-packed highway, cautious of panicked drivers. The spaceship became a small light in the sky behind them, dimming along with the bright city lights. No one stopped to offer them a ride.

"Everyone's fleeing," Josie said, eyeing the endless stream of cars with dismay. They weren't the only people on foot trudging alongside the highway. Perhaps Bane had been right to get them away when he did.

Bane grunted. He'd barely said two words to her since the altercation in the alley. Looking up at him, she hardly recognized the man she'd known.

It wasn't just his shaved head. His entire demeanor had changed.

"Where are we going?"

"Away," he replied.

"But where? You seem to have a plan." At least she *hoped* he had a plan and that it wasn't just to get as far away as possible.

"We'll stop soon."

"When?"

"When we've gone far enough."

Josie heard the agitation in his voice. Not wanting to anger him, she kept silent. But after another hour of walking and listening to Markley's steady meowing, she grew braver. "Maybe we could rent a car? I brought my purse—"

Bane stopped and spun around to glare at her. Josie froze at the look on his face. "And what? Go to an all-night car rental shop? And while we're at it, how about we stop for dinner and drinks?"

She knew he was being sarcastic, but dinner and drinks did sound good. She'd put the marinating steaks in the fridge—God only knew when they'd return—and she hadn't eaten since lunchtime. "I'm hungry and tired, and Markley's upset." It came out as a whine but too bad.

"Yeah, let's stop fleeing for our lives 'cause the cat's upset," Bane mocked her.

"What's your problem? Why are you being such an asshole all of a sudden?"

His furious expression made her take a step back. He reached out and grabbed her hand, and began to walk again. After they passed a young couple with a baby, Bane shot her a glance. "You don't seem to realize how serious this is."

"I can see it's serious," she protested, keeping her voice level. "I just want to know what we're doing." *And why you left an engagement ring forgotten on the floor.*

"There's a plan."

"What do you mean? Did they say something on TV about where we should go? Is that where everyone's going?" she asked.

"No. I just know. Me and some others know."

"You just know? What *others*? Who do you mean?" Every answer he gave her led to more questions.

"Don't worry. I have it under control," he said.

His tone held a warning not to push him. For the first time since she'd met Bane, she was afraid of him. Staying with him seemed her only option; she didn't have anyone else. She had no family. There were friends, but they may be fleeing as well.

Hours later, Bane decided they could rest. He settled them off to the side of the highway, deep in a grove of trees beside a stream. The gentle cascade of water offset the steady hum of the cars in the distance.

Josie opened Markley's crate and pushed a collar over his head. She snapped on a thin leash and let him wander out. He sniffed the air cautiously before roaming around. He drank a little of the water she scooped into his bowl from the stream and did his business before she coaxed him back into the crate.

"Get some rest." Bane had put down a blanket for them to lie on. He lay on his back, hands resting beneath his head. She settled down beside him, their bodies barely touching. The ground was hard beneath the blanket.

Josie turned on her side, her back to Bane, and stared into the dark trees. It was a mild evening, so she was comfortable in her jacket. Her feet ached, and she concentrated on the pain, letting it distract her from darker thoughts. It was a long time before she finally nodded into a restless sleep.

Before dawn, Bane was awake and urging her to get up. He handed her a sleeve of crackers to eat taken from a box he'd packed. After she'd eaten several, she got up and shook out the blanket. Bane took it from her, rolled it up, and put it back in the duffle bag.

"Let's go," he said.

No 'good morning, sweetheart,' or kiss. *Who the hell is this guy?* Josie took a moment of privacy for herself, then let the cat out for a wander and some food and water. Bane watched them with agitation. As soon as Markley was back in his crate, he marched them onward.

Back alongside the highway, Josie realized the traffic was even worse this morning—bumper to bumper, inching forward, horns blaring. The number of people traveling by foot had grown. Some cars had been abandoned, which only added to the congestion. Tempers flared. Shouts and foul language, along with shaking fists, shot from lowered windows in the growing heat. It appeared Bane wasn't the only one whose anger had crept to the surface.

Ahead of them, a crowd of people gathered in a carpool lot. As they got closer, Josie saw there were at least fifty of them. They had to pass the group, and as they walked by, Josie caught snatches of conversation.

"Another ship was spotted in Toronto," a woman said to the circle of people around her.

"I heard on the news they've arrived in almost every major city worldwide," said a bedraggled young man.

"Have they done anything yet besides sit there?" asked a young woman, her face streaked with mascara.

"Not that they've reported," answered the young man.

"I wonder what they want."

"Our water, I'm betting."

"The army is launching an attack. They'll scare them off."

"Yeah, right. They'll be annihilated just like the rest of us. It's an extermination, you'll see."

"They haven't done anything yet. Maybe they come in peace?"

Josie shuddered. She'd had similar thoughts to what these people feared or hoped. She supposed everyone's imagination was going wild. How frightening to think that several more ships had arrived. What *did* they want?

"We're waiting for a bus," an older lady said to Josie as Bane marched them past.

Josie stopped and turned to the woman. "A bus is coming here?"

"Yes," the woman replied. "That's why we're all standing here. It was on the radio. Buses are being sent along the highways, stopping at the carpool lots if people want a ride out of town."

Bane was tugging on her hand, but Josie pulled free. "Where's it headed? Is there someplace safe?"

The woman shrugged. "We're headed to Barrie. There's no ship there. At least not yet. As to if it's safe, we'll have to wait and see."

Josie turned to Bane. "We should go. If they're sending people there, they must think it's the best place to be right now."

"It isn't," Bane said, ignoring the older woman's stare. He latched onto Josie's hand to pull her away.

"Go to Barrie," the lady urged them. "It's our best chance."

Once they were past the group, Josie again broke free of Bane's grip. "Why can't we wait for the bus? Everyone else is going to Barrie. Why can't we?"

Bane gave her a chilling look. "Don't be a fool. If that's where the higher-ups are sending people, then it's definitely not the right place to go. They'll all be sitting ducks. Think about it."

What choice did she have? Was Bane right? Or was he leading them into more danger? She was tired and sick of walking. They never should have left home. Josie watched enviously as overfilled buses and steady rows of cars heading toward Barrie passed them by. Bane led them down the highway in the same direction, so she didn't know why they couldn't take one of the buses as well. It would've been a lot easier on the feet.

Just as the sun began to go down, they stopped at a motel for the night that was taking in guests.

Despite cringing at the smell and the questionable stains on the carpet, Josie thought it was heaven compared to sleeping outside. Markley was soon sprawled on the turquoise bedspread while she perched on the end of the bed, her gaze glued to the TV screen. It was true what she'd heard this morning—there were spaceships spotted over every major city in the world. *So many!*

Markley ducked under her arm and rubbed against her side. Josie stroked his sleek black fur. "Hungry, baby?"

She retrieved his bowls from the pack and filled one with his food. Bane was in the shower, so she would wait to get fresh water. Markley munched while Josie turned her attention back to the news.

When Bane came out of the bathroom, he had a small towel wrapped around his hips, his skin still glistening with beads of water. Josie felt an unexpected jolt of arousal. Strange, considering what was going on, how he could still turn her to jelly every time she saw his bare chest. The scowl he'd worn on his face since the invasion was ever present. Josie hoped their temporary indoor refuge would have a good effect on him.

She filled Markley's bowl with water and returned to perch on the bed while the cat lapped away and Bane dried off.

"See this?" Josie asked, pointing at the TV screen. "They're everywhere now."

"Yep." Bane dropped the towel and stretched out on the queen-sized bed.

Josie couldn't tell if the broadcast upset him or not. "I'm gonna shower."

He didn't look at her or say anything as she flounced off to the bathroom. When she returned, dried and naked, the room was dark and silent. As her eyes adjusted, she spotted the cat curled up in one of the chairs and surmised by the deep, even breaths coming from the direction of the bed that Bane was asleep.

Too bad. She'd been hoping to stoke the romantic embers. Not that their love life needed any rejuvenation; Bane's passion matched hers in every way. And yet, since the arrival of the UFOs—nothing. No kisses or hugs or long, lusty looks. Not even a comforting squeeze or a playful smack on the ass. She'd yet to broach the subject of the ring she found. He sure wasn't acting like a man ready to propose.

Josie lifted the edge of the blanket and slipped into bed. Bane lay on his back, arms up and crossed beneath his head. She stretched out beside him, turning to rest her head on his chest, and hitched her leg up over his. Out of habit, his arm came down to curl around her. Encouraged, Josie pressed a kiss to the light smattering of hair on his chest. She reached down past his belly and gently grasped him. He grew warm and hard as she stroked.

His hand moved to tangle in her hair. She reveled in the moment to have at last gained his attention. Despite his presence the past couple of days, she'd almost felt alone.

Bane's hips lifted slightly in motion, with her hand sliding up and down his hard length. Faster she moved. His head writhed back and forth across the pillow, his low moans grew louder, and his grip tightened in her hair. Soon he was pulling her up over his body. He held still for a moment, his warm, uneven breaths brushing her face.

Josie gasped as he suddenly rolled and flipped her beneath him. One strong leg pushed her thighs apart, and she felt him press up against her opening.

He took her hands and pulled them up over her head. In the next moment, he was surging forward, filling her with a bold thrust.

"Bane!" she cried. Though ready for him, she was shocked by the intensity with which he claimed her. Low pants escaped her, accenting his movements as he withdrew and plunged again and again. "Stop…" His passion frightened her and yet filled her with a primitive urge of her own. Her hips rose and fell, matching his rhythm.

"Must survive," he ground out between thrusts.

His words barely penetrated the fog in her brain as Josie fought for control. She wrestled her hands free of his grip and raked her nails down his back, causing him to dive even harder and deeper.

"Survive," he demanded, as though saying the word would enforce his will.

Josie cried out as spasms ripped through her. Slowly, she drifted back to reality, focusing on Bane as he thrust one last time and tensed. *Survive what?* His wild lovemaking?

* * * *

Bane knew his destination. Once they reached the

lake, a boat would be there waiting. It was located just outside a small town named Albion, a popular northern getaway which boasted several bodies of water. Where he was going was special, though. This lake would assure their survival. Several chosen sites around the world would be destinations for others like him and those they had brought with them.

He'd risen at dawn in preparation to leave as soon as possible. They didn't have the luxury of time. He was fully dressed, and their bags were packed. He'd even fed the damned cat.

"Wake up," he demanded.

Josie lingered in bed, curled around the sheets and pillows like her feline companion. Bane struggled to feel nothing as he watched the woman he'd loved more than life itself rub her eyes like a child and sit up in the bed they'd shared, her short, blonde hair tousled. They'd had sex last night, and he'd enjoyed it. After all of the tension the past couple of days, his body had craved release. When he'd sunk deep inside Josie's body and looked into her eyes, he'd stilled for a moment, feeling a part of him striving to break free—a part that wanted more than just sexual gratification.

Every aspect of their relationship was ingrained in his memories. He could flip through every single moment with impassive crystal clarity. Emotion had fought its way to the surface in that instant of their joining, but it was beaten back down by superior restraint. If they were going to survive, he had to remain focused. And withdrawn.

Josie rose to dress in clothing he'd left out for her. She took a few moments in the bathroom while he paced the floor and peered out the curtains toward the sky. She'd yet to say a word to him. Silence was good. It meant she was taking things seriously and was ready to accept their situation. There wasn't time to explain himself every five minutes to an emotional, unstable female. When she came out of the bathroom, he had the cat in its carrier and setting beside their bags at the door.

"Ready?" It was more of a command than a question.

"Yes." Her gaze settled on the cat carrier with noted relief. She moved forward, pulled on her boots, and picked up the carrier while Bane reached for the other bags. They went outside, Bane shut the door, and they didn't look back.

For hours they walked alongside the two-lane highway. Josie had sighed dramatically when they'd passed the exit to Highway 400, heading to Barrie. Using spare change, they'd raided what was left in the snack machine in the lobby of a motel along the way. Josie munched on a bag of chips, and he could hear her speaking calmly to the cat.

They'd hardly seen a soul for hours; even cars passing on the road had been few and far between. Bane figured that the majority of people who'd decided to pack up and flee had most likely already done so. It didn't matter where they went or what they did now. Everything they knew and understood about their world would soon be at an end. Time was running out for Earth, and unless they'd been lucky enough to bond with men like him, they'd be hard-pressed to survive.

They should reach their destination by sundown tomorrow. And by tomorrow night, he would secure their survival. Josie may not like what had to happen next, but he wouldn't give her the chance to object. He'd chosen her as his mate, and she would obey him regardless of how she felt. And whether here on Earth or someplace else, she would remain his.

CHAPTER 3

Alongside the road were three small, one-room cabins set a short distance from each other and the main house that rented them out. Using the last of their cash, Bane secured one of the cabins for their use. The owners, an old couple, conducted the transaction inside the foyer of their modest home. While Bane handed over the money and made small talk with the husband, Josie accepted with gratitude a seat on the hard bench and a hot cup of tea from the wife. Bane had refused the woman's offer of a beverage.

"It's all so strange," the old woman confided to Josie while taking a seat beside her. "We've heard reports about what's happening, and we've seen the steady stream of cars heading down the road, but I can't seem to accept that it's for real."

When Josie nodded her head politely, the woman asked her about the spaceships. "They're huge, gray and black, just hovering in the skies, terrifying, really. They appear to be targeting the main cities, as you've probably seen on the news."

"Yes, all over the world," the woman exclaimed.

"There was one in our town a few hours southwest of here. It's why we left. We passed by groups of people on the highway, and they were waiting for buses to take them to Barrie for safety."

"We heard about that too. Why didn't you go with them?"

Josie shrugged and glanced over at Bane. "He didn't agree."

The old woman smiled. "We didn't either. I say stay where you are. If these invaders are intelligent enough to fly all the way here, planning God knows what, then nowhere is safe. That is if they even mean us any harm. We don't know for sure. Perhaps they come in peace?"

Bane and Josie exchanged a look. Josie wasn't

about to tell this sweet, old couple about the gloomy prediction Bane had made. The man handed Bane a key and told him they could check out whenever they wanted tomorrow.

"It's not like people are lining up to rent," the man said with a strained smile.

Josie thanked the couple and headed outside with Bane toward the cabin. Night was just beginning to fall, and already she could see stars appearing in the sky. If she wasn't so exhausted, she might have suggested they enjoy a campfire in the small pit beside their cabin. Even if she wanted to, the cold look on Bane's face told her he wouldn't agree.

Inside, Josie freed Markley from his carrier and put out food and water for him. She placed their toiletries in the bathroom while Bane sat in one of the two chairs in front of the TV. She could overhear the newscaster, sounding tired and stressed out, telling the world that there'd been no change. The UFOs still hovered over the cities, their presence as curious and ominous as ever. Josie didn't know what was worse, the waiting or the inevitable outcome. As far as Bane was concerned, they were not here in peace.

Josie took a long, hot shower and then flipped through the channels while Bane took his turn in the bathroom. Nothing else was on—every single channel was dedicated to keeping an eye on the invaders and informing the public.

She was changing into her nightgown when the power went out.

"Bane?" Using the furniture for guidance, she stumbled toward the bathroom. She heard the door open and saw a tall, dark shape emerge.

"Jose?"

His use of her nickname caught her off-guard, had old Bane returned? She reached out, her hands coming in contact with Bane's still damp chest. "I don't know what happened. Everything went dark."

He took her hand and led her carefully over to the window to peer outside. Markley meowed, and she reached down to stroke the cat rubbing against her legs.

"Even the main house is out," Bane said. "I'm going to walk up there and see if they have a generator or a battery-powered radio." He led Josie over to the bed, and she watched his shadowy figure pull on his clothes. "Stay here," he said, heading for the door.

"Okay, hurry, though."

She was curled up on the bed with Markley when he returned a short time later.

She sat up and peered at him through the darkness. "Did you find out anything?"

He fiddled with something over at the side table. She heard a match strike and saw the glow of a small flame as he lit a couple of long candles set in little holders. "He's got a windup radio. Most stations have gone dark, but the others are running on generator power."

"Is it everywhere, then? Not just local?"

Bane came up to stand before the bed. When he spoke, the neutral tone of his voice gave Josie a chill. "The entire world's gone dark. This is the second wave, as I expected."

"What do you mean the second wave?"

"Arrival was the first," he said.

"What will happen next?" Her voice was barely a whisper. He seemed to know what was going on. How or why he possessed this knowledge was a mystery.

"I don't know for sure. Hopefully, it won't

happen for a while, at least another day or two."

"You think they're here to destroy us, don't you?"

"Yes." He didn't bother to sugarcoat it.

Josie held onto hope during the restless hours of the night that things may be better come morning. Though the power never came back on, at least they could see in the daylight.

As usual, Bane was up and dressed before her, impatient to be on their way. They only spared a few minutes to bid their hosts goodbye and good luck and then continue on down the highway. They stopped at a wide stream a few hours later to soak their feet and eat some of their snacks. Attached to his lead, Markley sat in the tall grass, keeping a sharp eye on insects.

"Where are we going, Bane?"

"We'll be there soon."

It frustrated her how he refused to answer most of her questions. If she pressed him, he shut down completely. She ran her fingers over the bump the ring made in the denim pocket of her jeans. Bane hadn't mentioned anything about proposing. Josie wasn't surprised, given what they'd endured, not to mention his strange behavior.

"Do you love me?" she suddenly asked him.

"What?" He stared at her.

"I said, 'do you love me'?" He'd been the first one in their relationship to say those words to her, and she'd heard it every day until the UFOs arrived.

When he shrugged and looked away, she sighed. Where exactly did things stand between them in this relationship now? Could she even call it a relationship any longer? Bane was intent on keeping her safe. That much was apparent. But the way he treated her suggested she was nothing more than important baggage.

Had he brought her with him out of a sense of obligation? Or was it something else? It certainly didn't seem like he acted out of love. She stared at his profile, searching for signs of instability. Maybe he'd lost all sense of reason and was acting on impulse? Was she right to blindly follow him? What other choice did she have?

Bane pulled on his socks and boots. Seeing his intention to leave, she did the same. She coaxed Markley back into his carrier and waited while Bane swung the backpack on and slung the other bag over his shoulder.

When he led them back onto the road, Josie
followed along silently.

* * * *

The sun was just beginning to set when they
reached the lake. Bane didn't question how he knew
exactly where to go and what to do. Awakening
to his purpose had been liberating. Strength and
decisiveness flowed through his veins like a divine
right.

"Why have we come here?" Josie asked.

He saw her shiver and didn't know if she
suffered from a chill or fear. Probably both. His
conscience reared up, and he thought of going
over and holding her, if only for a moment or two.
Annoyance battled with nostalgia and glimpses
of his old feelings that left him unsettled until the
Sentinel in him prevailed. He gazed across the
smooth surface of the small, circular lake and felt a
calm settle over him.

The boat was upside down and hidden in the
overgrown brush beside the water's edge several
yards away. He strode in its direction, knowing Josie
would follow. He could hear her clumsy footsteps

stumbling in haste behind him.

"Bane," she called. "What are you doing?"

He ignored her.

Reaching the boat, he cleared away several years' worth of brush, which almost obscured it from view. Once he finished, he flipped the boat over and untied an old, worn rope that secured it to a tree. Next, he pulled the boat to the lake's edge and pushed it into the water. He tossed the bags he carried onto its floor. He coiled the rope around his arm and placed that into the boat as well. Then he set the oars into place. It was a sturdy little rowboat—nothing extravagant, but it would get them to the middle of the lake.

Exactly where he needed them to be.

* * * *

Josie took a look at that boat, and one thought reared up in her mind. "Are you crazy?"

He had to be kidding. Bane didn't know how to even safely climb into a boat, never mind row one. If there was anything she knew and accepted about her man, it was that he was a city boy through and through. At least, he had been up until recently.

She took a step back when he reached for

Markley's carrier. "No."

"What do you mean *no*? Give me the damned cat and get in the boat." He was glaring at her again.

She backed up more. "I don't know what the hell you're doing, but I don't want any part of it."

Bane climbed into the boat, his sudden movements making it rock precariously. "I'm getting you to safety. That's what I'm doing."

"Safety is in Barrie, not here. Look around you! There's no one on this lake but us. No cottages, no nothing. I can't keep blindly following you like some fool. You have no idea what you're doing, do you?"

"You need to trust me."

Josie could see the intent burning in his eyes. Before the UFOs and before he turned Terminator, she would have believed in him, no questions asked. But now…. "I have trusted you for days. And look what it's gotten me—stuck in the middle of nowhere. We have no food, no money…." The ground beneath her feet suddenly vibrated and then shifted. The water rippled, and the boat rocked. "Bane?"

The look on his face frightened her; he didn't

appear shocked or worried, just resigned. The ground then shook so abruptly that she fell forward onto her hands and knees. Markley screeched as his carrier landed on its side. Josie heard cracking noises all around, followed by the sound of crashing. She lifted her head and scanned the forest. Trees were falling. Not just one or two, but several.

Bane was at her side in an instant, kneeling down, his arms around her. She looked into his eyes, and for once, they weren't bright with anger. The eyes staring at her now, filled with tenderness and concern, belonged to the man she knew, the man she loved.

"Come with me, Jose. Please," he said.

She nodded and allowed him to help her to her feet. The earthquake continued, knocking more trees down. Overhead, the sky rapidly darkened with eerie, black clouds flashing with lightning. Rain began to fall. "What's happening?"

"Third wave," he said, a large boom of thunder accenting his words. His look turned hard, once more masking the man she knew. He gripped her hand, and when she pulled away, he snatched up Markley's carrier and strode toward the water.

"Don't," she warned.

He put the carrier on the floor of the boat and climbed in. Arms crossed, he stared at her defiantly. "You have two choices. You either come with me." He raised his voice over the noise of the mounting storm. "Or you take your chances here."

Judging by the expression on his face, she knew he meant what he said. That son-of-a-bitch would leave her there. "You're a fucking asshole." She strode forward, ducked beneath his outstretched hand, and climbed into the boat. As she sat down on the front seat, she matched his hard look with one of her own. "Hope you know how to row, fucker."

He sat down and, to her surprise, began to row. They glided swiftly across the choppy waves that sloshed over the sides of the boat. He gauged his direction by peering over his shoulder. Though she fumed, she was also amazed at the ease and skill he displayed with the oars. She longed to ask him about his newly acquired ability, but more pressing worries bombarded her. What did he mean about the third wave? Was he actually implying the UFOs had something to do with the storm and the earthquakes? How could that be possible? Causing a blackout was one thing, but messing with nature was quite another.

She braced Markley's carrier between her feet, grit her teeth, and pulled the hood of her jacket up over her head. The waves grew in size as the earthquakes continued, and she worried about trees crashing into them if they crossed the lake and tried to dock on the other side.

But that didn't appear to be Bane's plan. When they reached the middle of the water, he stopped rowing and let go of the oars. Maybe he feared the falling trees, and he figured they were safest far from shore? He got to his feet.

"Whatever happens, stay put," he said, and then dove over the side of the boat.

"Bane!"

She went down on her knees and reached out, scrambling to find him in the dark water, but he'd gone deep, and there was no sign of him. She screamed his name over and over until her voice grew hoarse.

"Why did you leave me?" she whispered. They'd come so far together, so why now? Exhausted, she slumped against the side of the boat and waited.

Remarkably, the boat remained where he'd left it despite the waves determined to push it back to shore. He hadn't anchored it, Josie reflected; the only rope she saw lay coiled on the floor. The rain continued to pour down, and the world around her still erupted in chaos.

How could you leave me here?

How long she remained sitting numbly, hearing the frightened cries of Markley over the howl of the wind and the thunder, she had no idea. So when a light appeared beneath the surface, and a wide, dark shape began to rise up, she stared at it in shock. "What the hell?"

Slowly, the object surfaced. She noted it was sleek and black, about eight or more feet high by about ten feet long, saucer-shaped, resembling a miniature version of the UFOs floating over the cities. A moment later, she saw a hidden panel whisk upward, revealing a doorway. Bane stood in the opening.

"Bane?" She stared at him in wonder.

The craft rested barely five feet from the boat. "Reach the oar out to me, and I'll pull you over," he instructed.

She found herself mechanically obeying. The sight of him, knowing he was safe, overcame any reservations she harbored. He caught the oar and pulled her toward him.

"The cat," he said.

"Oh, yeah." *Did I actually forget Markley?*

He put the carrier inside the craft and then took the other bags she passed to him. Then he reached for her hand.

She caught a glimpse over his shoulder of a high-tech panel with flashing lights. A domed, circular podium, about waist high, dominated the center of the space.

He pulled her up and moved aside, giving her room to enter. The door whisked shut, closing them inside. She looked around in wonder.

"How?" The first question that came to mind.

"There's a lot to explain. First, we need to head someplace safe."

He led her over to a pair of high-back chairs, and she sat down. He took up a stance before the podium and peered down intently as though searching for something. Sets of controls encircled the miniature dome. He pushed a few buttons and flipped a couple of switches, causing the dome to glow. Across from her, she saw a section of the ship vibrate and then become transparent, allowing her to see outside.

Bane came over and sat down in the seat beside her. As the craft lifted up off the surface of the water, he reached for her hand. Very soon, the tops of the trees disappeared, and all she could see was the starry night sky. She knew they were moving, but she'd yet to feel any motion.

She stared down at her hand clinging tightly to Bane's. Lifting her gaze to his, she was dismayed at seeing the stranger she'd spent the last few days with and not the man she'd fallen in love with. It dawned on her that he probably hadn't taken her hand in comfort. More likely, it was to keep her from fleeing.

CHAPTER 4

This is it, Josie thought. Bane was taking her to one of the huge ships in the sky. He was the enemy, and she'd blindly followed him right to her own demise. The words *take me to your leader* echoed in her head. She stifled the urge to give in to crazed laughter. How could she have been so trusting? So stupid?

"Are you one of them?" she asked, her voice barely a whisper.

"No." His chilly gaze suggested otherwise.

Carefully, she disentangled her fingers from his and tried to scoot over in her seat. His eyes narrowed.

"I'm not one of them," he insisted.

She stared around the ship's interior, vainly searching for a way out.

"Jose." His voice was gentle, but she wasn't fooled.

"I know what this is. It's like *Invasion of the Body Snatchers*." Josie got to her feet and glared at him accusingly. If she was going down, she'd go down fighting. And knowing the truth.

He actually laughed. "God, this is my fault for making you watch that damned movie a million times with me."

Josie peered at him intently. Yes, he looked like Bane. And when he tried really hard, he could even act like Bane. But he wasn't him. He couldn't be him. She waved her hand. "You don't fool me. Not anymore. I should have seen it earlier. All the signs were there. The coldness, the detachment, you don't even like the cat."

"I saved the damn cat," he argued.

"Grudgingly, and only so you could get me to go with you. So what happens now, huh? You take me up to the ship, and some alien asshole inhabits my body too?"

"Calm down." He exhaled loudly and ran a

hand over his head.

"Don't tell me to calm down. You've kidnapped me, and now you're taking me up there—"

"I'm not taking you to the alien ship," he interrupted.

"Then where are you taking me?"

He reached out his hand, and Josie took a step back. "Don't touch me."

"I haven't been replaced by a pod person."

"Yeah, well, prove it," she snapped.

He stared at her for several moments. A coy smile crossed his lips as though he recalled something amusing. "Do you remember how we got Markley?"

"Yes, of course. Do you?"

He chuckled, then frowned as though annoyed with himself. "We weren't looking for a pet. We'd talked about getting one once we saved up enough money to buy a house. But then, we wanted a dog."

Josie nodded but wasn't taken in so easily.

"I was writing my fourth novel. You were at my old apartment making us dinner, and I was working. I came out of the den and asked you to come to listen to something."

She didn't say anything, only waited for him to continue.

"There was scratching in the walls. You didn't hear it, so I got you to kneel down behind my desk. Remember you told me the sound was in my head. That maybe I needed to take a break. But then you heard it too. You tapped on the drywall, and we both heard a little cry. I dug a hole out with a knife, further down from the noise, so I wouldn't hurt whatever it was. You stood back by the door, afraid it was a rat, or a mouse, or something sinister. And then, out popped this tiny, black head meowing its face off. We named him Markley, after the alien in my story."

Josie wiped a tear that came to her eye. When he held out his hand again, she went to him. He pulled her into his arms, and she rested her head on his chest.

The sky was so much darker, the stars so much brighter since the blackout. Now that her initial shock had passed, Josie felt millions of questions brimming over inside of her. Whether her companion cared to answer them or not would be another matter.

Markley meowed loudly, and she asked Bane if she could let him out. He agreed, and she knelt down to open the carrier. The cat appeared unfazed; after sniffing around a bit, he curled up and began washing his paws.

Bane moved around the small interior of the ship, opening and closing several hidden compartments. From each, he extracted a palm-sized, metallic device that was high-tech in appearance. He put a couple of them into his jacket pockets and the others into the bags they'd brought on board. Ignoring her sodden clothes, she retook her seat and gave her companion a quizzical gaze, hoping he'd take the hint.

Eventually, Bane sat down and ran his hand over his shaved head. She waited patiently while he appeared to gather his thoughts. "Earth is under attack. We've known this day would come eventually."

"We?" she asked.

"There are others like me. We're here because of them."

"You're not like them—the ones in the

ships?" Her tone sounded stilted. She rubbed her sweaty palms on her damp jeans.

"No. Well, yes. In some ways." He exhaled a long breath. "How can I explain this in a way you'll understand?"

"Start at the beginning," she suggested. Absentmindedly, she trailed her fingers through her wet hair.

"I'm not human."

"What? What do you mean?" *God, if he starts shedding his skin…*

"I appear human, the others like me do as well, but we're actually from another planet—"

"Wait a sec." She gripped her hands together; that crazed laughter threatened to bubble up, and she had to force herself to get control. So he wasn't a pod person. They'd established that. But this was worse. It took several deep breaths before she knew she could speak calmly. "Have you known this all along? Because you're sure a damn convincing actor if you did."

"No, I didn't, not until the invasion. It was like a switch turned on, awakening me, and suddenly I remembered everything. Remembered who I am."

Josie looked at her hands and saw they were trembling. "And who is that?"

"We're Acacians from Planet Gannon. Those of us who are here, we're what you would call Sentinels—guardians of Earth. Protectors of the human race."

"Against what?"

"Extinction."

She surged to her feet. This was all too much. "You mean those ships….they're here to wipe us out—completely?" Deep down, she'd feared exactly that. Yet, part of her had prayed she was wrong.

"Eventually, yes." He didn't bother to sugarcoat it.

"So that's how you knew about the waves—the arrival, the electricity, the earthquakes. My God! How are they doing this? Why are they doing this?" *I can't believe I've been having sex with an alien!*

"As advanced as you think Earth is, in comparison to them, you're nothing. Humans have no idea what they're up against and can't possibly hope to compete. These invaders—I'm certain they're Cadeyrns, from Planet Centeris—can cause earthquakes and manipulate the weather, but it's just the beginning. They're capable of much more. This is like a game to them. They'll sit up there in the ships and wreak havoc until they tire of it. Then they'll come down here and pick off whoever's left."

"Why Earth? What do they want?"

"Water, resources, whatever they can use. Planets like yours are few and far between. And Earth is an easy conquest."

"They could ask for help. I'm sure humans would rather share everything rather than have it taken from us."

"They don't ask. They take. Humans are merely an obstacle they need to eliminate. They've done it before."

"But you said you're here to help. You can stop this, right? Tell me you can stop them."

He shrugged. "We'll do what we can."

"*What you can?* That doesn't sound reassuring."

He gave her a cold look, causing her to take a step back. "For approximately every two hundred and fifty thousand humans, there is one of us. We're scattered all over the planet. Judging by the number of ships out there, I'd say the invaders outnumber my kind at least six to one."

"If your kind knew this day was coming, why aren't there more of you? Are more coming?"

"I don't know. Even if they could get here in time, they might be too late. And as to your other question...it's no easy thing leaving your world behind to safeguard another. Those of us who are here are descendants of those who have walked the Earth alongside humans since the beginning. Originally, a large number of us volunteered to remain and keep humans and the Earth safe. I was born here. My father was an Acacian, as was his father and his father before him, and so on. Though they never knew their true identity, there was no need. We hoped we would be enough."

Josie couldn't believe they'd been here all along. "So what's the plan? Is there one?"

"Their ships are superior to ours—these small crafts we have on Earth. We cannot engage them until they descend."

"So we have to take whatever they dish out until they come down?" The frustration she felt was evident in her tone.

"Yes."

* * * *

Josie slumped down in her seat. "I can't believe this is happening."

Bane didn't feel the need to give her reassurance, not when he couldn't be certain of the outcome. His objective was to keep as many humans alive as possible. If total annihilation seemed imminent, then he was to take his mate and leave Earth. But he wasn't about to relay that part of the plan unless it became necessary. Other Acacians had the same objective. They, too, would remain with their mate, secure a small town, and hope to save as many as possible. If their town fell, they would take their mate and leave.

The point that he'd failed to mention, in order to spare Josie some fear, was that the Cadeyrns would take more than food and resources. They'd take slaves as well, as many as they could fit aboard their ships. Men to mine the miniscule resources left deep beneath the surface of Centeris, and women to use in depraved sexual acts. Cadeyrn women, being the more dominant sex, only allowed mating when a child was to be conceived. Other than that, the men were forced to leave them alone. The men also outnumbered the women about a hundred to one, making copulation a far-reaching fantasy to the sexually frustrated males.

The knowledge of the enemy Bane possessed was current down to minute details, downloaded into his head along with all pertinent information. Somehow or another, his brain must have connected to a collective knowledge bank, frequently updated by Gannon over the years. Bane wished he were able to tap into a collective mind and communicate with other Sentinels and those on Gannon, but he couldn't. He could only hope that the awakening Sentinels would perhaps activate a warning alarm, alerting Acacians to the danger Earth faced.

He looked over at Josie and saw her eyes close. Everything about her screamed exhaustion. Despite the journey they'd endured, he felt far from exhausted. Exhilarated was more like it. Purpose pumped through his veins.

Earth was under attack, but he was not overly distressed about it. Not when it meant freedom from his inferior self. Though he now knew his true identity, there were still underlying traces of the man he'd thought himself to be.

That man had been the one to reassure Josie he was still the same person she knew and loved. Reliving the memory about Markley had been a trial, yet also a necessity considering the circumstance. The Sentinel in him had allowed it, if only to avoid having a hysterical female on his hands. A flicker of that man had also emerged when Josie fell at the lake. For the briefest of seconds, he'd let down his guard and felt emotions that should have remained buried. Sentiment he acquainted with weakness, and it had no place in the here and now. In order to carry out his mission, he must hold a tight rein. He was resolved to do so no matter the cost.

* * * *

From the window, Josie noticed their descent. Clouds in the sky had cleared enough to allow the moon to cast a dim glow over the ground below. To her surprise, they seemed to be aiming toward another small lake. "Are we landing?"

"Yes."

She shivered, recalling how the ship had emerged from the bottom of a lake. "You're not putting it down *in* the water, are you?" *Markley will freak.*

"No, in the forest. We'll be staying close by."

This surprised her. "We are?"

"There's a cabin. It belonged to my dad. My grandfather owned the land originally."

"Really? Have you ever been there?" She hadn't recalled him mentioning it.

Bane actually smiled. "I'd forgotten about it. Now that things have come back to me, I remember my dad taking me there a couple of times when I was young. Just him and me. He said it was tradition. His dad took him camping on the land and always talked about building a cabin there. My dad did more than talk about it. He actually built the cabin."

"What about your mom? Did she ever go there with you?"

He shook his head. "No, I don't think she knew anything about it. My grandmother, either. Makes sense considering they're human."

That was interesting. "So you're actually half-human."

He frowned as though the thought had just occurred to him. "Yeah, I guess so."

"It's strange how your dad and grandfather didn't know they were aliens, yet they had a secret cabin waiting in the wings just in case," Josie said. Another thought struck her. She knew Bane was an only child, but what about others like him? "Are all of you who are born to an Acacian father an only child and a son? No daughters?"

"Always sons. And yes, no siblings."

"Interesting. So you need human females to reproduce?"

"The Sentinels do as a way of necessity since there are no Acacian females on Earth."

"So, do all Acacians look like humans? Or just the Sentinels?"

He seemed to ponder her question for a moment as though he was mentally searching for the answer. "From all outward appearance, we resemble humans. Physically, there are no discerning differences. It's our superior brains that are different."

Josie ignored the barb. "It's so weird that humans have said for years that aliens exist among us. They're always described as having a big head, giant eyes, and frail little bodies." Which Bane obviously had none of. "Like, look at the aliens you write about. I don't remember you ever having them resemble humans." It was strange, now that she thought about it, how he used to write about aliens. All the time she'd known him, he'd been fascinated by them, as though, deep down, they'd shared some strange connection.

"There are aliens that look like that," he informed her. "Not many, though, and the ones that do are mostly interested in studying humans. They don't pose a threat."

She thought for a moment. "So, why do Acacians care about humans? Don't get me wrong, I'm glad you do, but why? Or is it just the Earth you want to protect?"

He exhaled loudly as though he was getting bored with all her questions. "It's a long story. The short version is, thousands of years ago, an Acacian ship crash-landed on Earth. Two men were aboard. Both were hurt, but the small village they landed near took the men in and cared for them. One of the Acacians fell in love with a village girl. When help finally came from Gannon, he decided to remain on Earth. The other man who'd been in the crash left but vowed he'd return to Earth one day. He was best friends with the one who decided to stay. He did return with several men who decided they'd like to live on this strange, new planet."

He paused for a moment.

"The men on Gannon outnumber the women. It's the same on several planets. Don't ask me why. It just is. Anyway, the chance for a new life presented itself. In return for humans' hospitality, we helped them to advance. Back then, Earth was even less prepared for a hostile alien attack than it is now. Over the years, several more Acacian men arrived, spreading out all over the planet, vowing to keep Earth and the men and women who live here safe. Over the years, as generations of Acacian and human offspring lived and died, the memories and stories of the arrival of the Acacians were forgotten. The knowledge of who we were was buried deep in our minds, only to be awakened when the time came. Now is that time."

Josie was fascinated. But before she could ponder more on the subject, Bane swooped the craft low to the ground toward a small clearing in a thick forest. The ship hovered over the ground but did not set down.

He got to his feet. "Put Markley in his crate,

and we'll go."

She did as he instructed, and when he saw the cat was secure, he shouldered the bags and palmed a small, pulsing circle beside the hatch. The doorway swished up, and he jumped the couple of feet to the ground. He turned and put up his hand for Markley. Josie handed him the carrier and jumped to the forest floor that was slick with wet leaves. The hatch swished closed behind her.

Rain continued to fall in a slight drizzle. She was relieved to see that, although several trees had been knocked down, the ground no longer shook with tremors. Bane pulled one of the devices he'd gotten from the ship out of his jacket pocket. He gripped the hand-sized instrument in both his palms and twisted the top and bottom parts in opposite directions until a click sounded, causing it to light up like a beacon.

"Let's go," he said, striding into the thickness of the forest, taking for granted she would follow along.

She sighed and did just that. It'd been an incredibly long and exhausting day—a few days, actually—and she couldn't wait for it to be over. She hoped the cabin he led them to would be comfortable and safe. Although, how safe could they expect to be and for how long?

"By tomorrow, the Cadeyrns may begin their descent," Bane warned. "They have a weapon especially made for ground use. It can incinerate almost a dozen people at a time. The device is genius. There'll be no bodies rotting in the streets, causing sickness or contaminating food or water supplies."

She didn't know to respond. He seemed to bear no sentiment about the devastation of humanity—strange considering he'd so recently believed himself to be one of them. The thought of the world's population being annihilated was terrifying. Billions of men, women, and children, entire cities and communities, destroyed. How would they ever recover from something so terrible? Were they even meant to recover, or was this the end?

"The Cadeyrns' ships are over all the major cities. That's where they'll concentrate their attacks. The smaller towns are not of consequence to them—yet. Their main goal is to eliminate as much of the population as possible in the shortest amount of time. We'll do whatever we can to prevent total annihilation."

Josie shivered, thinking how very close they'd been to the heart of the chaos. Despite Bane's cold and calculating ways, he'd actually saved her life. She ached inside for the eventual loss of the others but didn't know of any way to prevent it.

Soon the forest began to thin, and the dark shape of a structure emerged ahead. "There it is," Bane announced.

Markley meowed several times as though sensing comfort and freedom from his confines. They came up before the cabin, and Josie thought it looked cozy. It sat on the point of a small lake, isolated by miles of thick forest. No light from candles, flashlights, or any other source was visible around the shore, so she surmised this was the only structure here.

As though reading her mind, Bane said, "It sits on a hundred acres. Most of the land around the lake, which is named Bentley, is Crown land. It's owned by the government."

He climbed the three steps to the deck and set the bags down. Reaching up atop a light fixture beside the door, he withdrew a key. He propped the screen door open with his knee. After he unlocked the wooden door, he swung it inward and shone his light inside. Josie came up beside him. From the warm, stale air that rushed out, she figured it'd been closed up for a long time. Bane grabbed the bags and entered the cabin. She followed him in and shut the door.

"Wait here," he said, setting down the bags again.

Josie put Markley's carrier on the floor and stood in the kitchen. Bane grabbed a set of keys and went back out the door, leaving her in the dark. Following the glow of his light with her eyes, she watched him walk over to the wooden shed attached to the cabin and open the door. Moments later, the light in the kitchen came on. She was surprised. It didn't appear to be powered by propane, and she couldn't hear the telltale sound of a generator. Bane soon came back inside and began switching on more lights.

"How'd you get the power on?" she asked, hoping that maybe the electricity had miraculously come back on and he had simply thrown the power switch.

"Alien power supply out in the shed. Once it's on, it's on. No electricity, gas, diesel, or propane needed."

"Cool. Can I let Markley out now?" When he nodded, she opened the carrier and fished the cat's bowls out of one of the bags. She filled a bowl with his dry food and took the other to the sink in the kitchen. "Is this water safe to drink?" She turned on the faucet and waited while the pipes groaned to life and water sputtered out in a drizzle from the tap.

"Yeah, it's from a deep well. It should be fine. Let it run for a while. It's full of air bubbles. I'll turn on the taps in the bathroom and let them run too."

Josie waited a bit and then filled up the water bowl before shutting off the tap. She set the bowl down beside Markley, who was munching away on his food, tail swishing rapidly back and forth. "I'm glad there's indoor plumbing," she said as Bane reentered the living room.

Now that the cabin was lit up, she could see everything more clearly. The kitchen was small. A counter acted as a divider between it and the living room. Four doors led off the living room, which was a good size. She figured two were bedrooms, one a bathroom, and the last being another access to outside. A stone fireplace nestled in the corner. The furniture consisted of two comfy chairs and a couch, all appearing to be from the seventies. The walls were paneled, and the carpet was shag. There was peel-and-stick tile on the floor in the kitchen. Despite having felt like she'd stepped back in time, Josie found the cabin comfortable and neat, besides needing a good airing out and dusting.

Markley finished up his food while Josie turned off the taps in the bathroom and went around opening up all the windows, letting in the cool night air. Bane took their bags into the largest bedroom, which had a long dresser and a cedar chest at the base of the queen-sized bed. The smaller bedroom had a dresser and bunk beds. Both rooms had serviceable deep green carpets and dark green curtains covering two windows.

"Does that door lead outside?" she asked.

Bane went over and pulled the door open, and gestured for her to come see. "Watch that the cat doesn't get out," he said, opening up a screen door that led to a large deck facing the tip of the point.

Through the trees, Josie could detect the dark water of the lake surrounding them on three sides. She stood beside Bane, who leaned against the rail of the deck, staring out at the water. The warm night and the lulling sounds of bullfrogs and crickets made her smile. She linked her arm with Bane's and leaned against him. For just a moment, she wanted to pretend that everything was all right. That there were no spaceships lurking around determined to decimate Earth. That Bane was the same man she'd known and loved for two years. And that the ring in her pocket would one day be on her finger.

Bane moved back abruptly. "Let's go in. We can eat, have sex, then sleep. Early tomorrow, I need to leave for a while." Without waiting for a response, he strode inside.

Josie sighed and waited to go in, preferring her own company to his. Every time she thought they were reconnecting, he turned back into a bastard.

CHAPTER 5

Bane was rifling through the cupboards when Josie came inside. He'd taken off his jacket. Josie removed hers and tossed it over his on the back of one of the chairs. Markley was curled up, washing himself by the fireplace in the other chair. Josie went into the kitchen area and swung her leg over the bench of the polished picnic table that served as the kitchen table.

"None of the food here will be edible," she informed him. "Not if it's been sitting in this furnace for the past fifteen to twenty summers."

"I know. I'm taking stock of what I need to grab in town. Will you go through the bags and see if there's anything left to eat?"

She climbed back off the bench and went into the bedroom. The bags were sitting on the floor. She found the last sleeve of crackers and a couple tins of chicken noodle soup and brought them into the kitchen.

"This is it," she said, putting the food on the counter.

She rinsed out two bowls and boiled water for tea—there were some ancient tea bags stashed inside a jar in the cupboard she figured wouldn't kill them. Soon, Bane had the soup heated. He filled their bowls while Josie finished making the tea, and they sat down across from each other.

As she ate, she watched him. He stared straight ahead and didn't make eye contact. She wondered about the remark he'd made about sex. He hadn't raised an eyebrow, given her a wink, or shown any indication he was hot for her. She wasn't exactly hot for him, either. Especially after all he'd told her.

She tried to put herself in his position. He could be confused and overwhelmed. Realizing his purpose in life was to act as guardian for another race and planet probably contributed to his foul temper. Maybe she could get him to open up. When he thought he was human, he'd shared everything with her—his thoughts and feelings, his hopes and dreams.

"I can't imagine how you're feeling. It's a huge weight on your shoulders, knowing your role is to prevent the destruction of an entire race. It must be disturbing to realize you're not who you thought you were after all this time."

The eyes he turned on her were impassive. "What does that have to do with anything? I have a mission to carry out, and I will. My personal feelings don't register in this."

"But they should. You have every right to be angry. I know you must be wondering about your own people and your own planet. Maybe part of you wants to get in your spaceship and go home. I know I would."

"I would never abandon my mission. The thought would never occur to me." A few minutes later, he gestured at her near-empty bowl. "Are you finished?"

"Why, are you ready for sex now?" She didn't bother to keep the sarcasm out of her voice.

He gave her a blank stare. "Yeah, I'm anxious, and it'll burn off some pent-up energy. Help me to concentrate."

"Glad I can be of service." While she wanted to yell and scream at him, anything to get some kind of response, she reined in her anger instead. Yelling at him was only going to make him angry. He'd mentioned he was leaving in the morning. She didn't want their remaining time together to be spent arguing.

Making a decision, Josie stood up and sauntered into the bedroom. She could hear Bane crossing the room behind her. She stood at the side of the bed and boldly faced him. Keeping eye contact, she peeled her still-damp shirt up and over her head, letting it fall to the floor. Then she unlaced her boots and kicked them off. She shimmied out of her pants and tossed them aside. Then she unhooked her bra and tossed that aside as well.

Bane reached for her tits, and his gentle squeeze surprised her. He ran his thumbs over her nipples, making them harden into tight buds. She gave him a seductive smile but got no response. His muscles bulged through the fabric of his shirt. Josie reached out to run her fingertips down the length of him. Moving her fingers underneath his shirt, she lifted it slowly to bare his stomach and chest. He helped her pull it off, and it went sailing across the room. Next, she turned her attention to his pants.

The wet denim stuck to him like a second skin. Unzipping his jeans, she could feel his erection through his briefs, straining against her hands. He was hot for her now despite the cold, restrained look on his face. Josie was determined to see his eyes flare with lust before she finished with him. She dropped to her knees and pulled his jeans down past his ass to his ankles. Bane stepped out and used one of his feet to toss them across the floor.

She pulled his briefs down to the floor, letting him kick them aside. He suddenly lifted her and tossed her onto the bed. He stared at her for a moment before he reached for her panties and pulled them off. He bent down and put his lips to her nipple, making her back arch in delight. Moments later, he moved his hips between her legs and drove deep inside of her, only to withdraw and plunge again. His eyes closed, his jaw tensed in concentration. She wondered what he was thinking about and felt certain it wasn't loving tender thoughts. Despite her grim ponderings, an orgasm ripped through her suddenly. Bane pushed deep inside her and stilled, reaching his own peak.

As she slowly drifted back to Earth, she saw Bane's eyes upon her. A slight smile touched his lips that Josie felt relayed the sentiment *triumphant*. She thought she'd led this dance of seduction. Instead, the tables had turned, and he had conquered her.

Later, as they lay there in the dark and Bane's soft snores filled the room, Josie climbed out of bed and reached for her pants. Digging into the deep pocket, she withdrew the ring. She tiptoed across the room, eased open the bottom drawer of the dresser, and stashed the ring inside. Tomorrow after he left for whatever it was he had to do, she would unpack their bags. Then she'd set about tidying up the cabin, which was to be their home for God only knew how long. She climbed back into bed beside Bane. Her mind turned to thoughts of their little apartment.

Home. What was that now? A building in the middle of a city filled with chaos, which was about to get a lot worse. Leaving had, of course, been the better option. Earth was about to change for the worse. She didn't want to imagine what was happening there right now or what else would soon happen. Like it or not, they were here to stay. She only prayed that they'd be safe and survive what was to come.

* * * *

The next morning when Josie awoke, Bane was already out of bed and getting ready to leave. Quickly, she got dressed and joined him in the kitchen. He had gone through their bags and set on the table an array of high-tech devices he'd removed from the ship. He was turning and twisting each one like a Rubik's Cube and snapping pieces into place. Once he'd finished with one, he would set it down and wait as it emitted a faint hum and pulse of light, then he'd carry on with the next one. She had no idea of their purpose, and she wasn't about to ask him for any information. Not with that crabby, purpose-filled look on his face.

She busied herself, feeding the cat and stroking his soft fur while Bane dumped out everything from his backpack and started filling it with his alien stuff. He went into the small bedroom and returned with a wad of cash that he folded up and tucked in his pocket. She didn't question him about it. His father had most likely left it there just in case. If they hadn't been under attack now, Josie figured Bane would, at some point, restock the horde of cash with fresh bills for the next generation.

"I'm not sure how long I'll be." He sat down at the table to lace up his boots.

"Are you getting supplies?"

"That and some other stuff."

"Like what?" She cringed at the scowl on his face, wondering if he'd tell her.

He got to his feet and shouldered the bag. "If everything goes as planned, I won't be long. Stay close to the cabin. There shouldn't be any trouble here yet, but don't take any chances."

Okay, then.

He went out the door without another word. Josie watched as his swift strides took him down the driveway and off into the forest. He headed in the same direction they'd come from last night.

Markley turned circles around her legs, and she bent down to scoop him up. "Where's Daddy going?" The cat purred in response.

She wondered if Bane was going to the spaceship. Maybe he planned on flying it into town? She could just imagine the response he'd get. The townspeople would probably stone him, though, with that thick head of his, he probably wouldn't feel it.

"I bet he parks that thing right in the grocery store parking lot and goes in to shop. Wouldn't that be something?" She carried the cat into the bedroom and began to put all of her and Bane's things into the dresser, making sure to pile her clothes on top of the ring she'd hidden.

* * * *

Bane strode through the woods in the direction of his ship. On the way, he'd stopped at the first signal point and set one of the protegats from his bag in place. Combined, there were seven that needed to be placed in position. When all of them were set, the town's safety would be assured. By now, the Cadeyrns would have descended into the cities to initiate the elimination stage. He still had time but not a lot of it.

Once on his ship, he set off to the other signal points and positioned a protegat in each. Afterward, he landed his ship on the outskirts of town and grabbed his now-empty backpack before heading out on foot. He'd have to travel back and forth from the ship with his purchases since he wouldn't be able to carry everything at once.

On his third trip back, a sudden flash of memory bombarded him. He and Josie had been Christmas shopping. With their tight schedules, he thought it'd be a good idea to finish off their lists in one day, and Josie had been up for the challenge. Taking things seriously, he'd even rented a car to carry everything. Back and forth they'd gone, shopping and unloading their purchases over the next several hours, only stopping for lunch and then again for dinner. They'd done it, though, he recalled, with lots of laughter and handholding. Their lists were relatively short, considering they were both only children and neither had living parents. Most of the gifts were for friends, business acquaintances, and each other. That night they'd shared a bath and a bottle of wine, taking turns rubbing each other's aching feet. Then they'd made love....

He shook his head to dislodge the memory. Looking around, he found himself standing in the middle of a strip of forest where he'd hidden the ship, dazed like a love-struck fool. What was the matter with him, he wondered angrily. There was no time to waste on sentimentality. The days of the past were over. He needed to be strong now and in the days ahead. Soon, everyone in this town would be relying on him. He had to present himself as a leader, possessing veritable strength and decisiveness, or he'd be facing rebellion and mass panic. Granted, there were only about twenty-five hundred people in town, yet once it was completely sealed off from the outside world, there'd be a lot of fear and speculation. He had to be ready to address the crowds who'd be looking for answers.

"Are you all right?" The sound of a young man's voice broke his concentration.

Still holding the heavy bags in his grip, Bane turned around slowly. The man staring at him was in his mid-twenties, he guessed, with a small build, glasses, and an intelligent face.

"I'm fine," Bane answered smoothly, even managing to smile a little.

"Taking a shortcut?"

"Yeah."

"Pretty wild what's going on, don't you think? I can hardly believe it." When Bane merely stared at him, the man rambled on. "We've been lucky here. I guess our small town doesn't pose a threat to them." Still no reaction. "You're smart to stock up. With the power out, most of the stores won't stay open for long. Even the ones with generators are only open for half a day or less." The man smiled tightly and gazed around, clearly grasping for something else to say. His eyes suddenly opened wide, staring off to his right. "What is that?"

Goddamn it! He'd seen the ship of all the dumb luck to have run into someone here and now. Bane put down his bags. "I dunno," he said, maneuvering closer to the stranger in the ruse of trying to get a better look at the ship.

He couldn't have this jackass freaking out and alerting everyone. There'd be a mass exodus out of town. He needed as many people as possible to remain within the vicinity. He'd been careful to keep the ship low and to remain in thickly treed areas to avoid detection.

The man crept closer and closer toward the ship. "Holy shit. Do you think this is part of the invasion? Maybe they sent smaller ships to the smaller towns? They probably don't have the ability to hover for long periods of time—" His voice cut off as he suddenly slumped to the ground.

Bane dropped the fist-sized rock he'd been holding. He checked the man's pulse and made sure he still breathed. He didn't want him dead, just out of the way for now. Once he woke up, it would be too late, his plan would be put into motion, and nothing and no one could stop it.

* * * *

Josie sat on the dock with her bare feet dangling in the water. A canoe rested upside down in the tall grass near the water's edge. She'd finished dusting the cabin, and having left the windows open all night, the air was definitely fresher. She could hear Markley's loud meows coming from the cabin. The poor thing had been pacing restlessly all morning, letting her know of his displeasure. Whatever had him on edge seemed to be wearing on her as well. It was as though the very air was filled with tension since Bane had gone out.

She pondered his words about the Sentinels being among them since the beginning—a veritable alien safeguard. He hadn't been very forthcoming in regards to information about the Acacians. Nor did he know if Gannon would send anyone else to help defend Earth. She wondered what would happen if Acacians did arrive. No doubt there'd be a huge battle with enormous destruction. A preferable outcome compared to the alternative—the end of the human race.

If the Acacians were victorious, the human survivors would be left to pick up the pieces and try to rebuild the world and their lives. It wouldn't be easy. Afterward, when the dust cleared, would the Acacians remain and help aid the survivors? Or would they leave and let humans deal with the aftermath alone? Would the Sentinels leave as well? What if they all decided to remain and take control of the planet, thinking humans incapable of defending it?

As much as she wanted answers to her questions, she feared Bane would tell her nothing. After all, he may not have any idea about what the Acacians would do after the fighting was over—if they arrived at all. He'd lived on Earth his entire life and would probably feel like a stranger to his own kind.

She recalled the night they met. They had literally bumped into each other going into a restaurant. Since both planned on dining alone, Bane suggested they share a table. He'd been twenty-four, she twenty-one, her parents dead a little under a year. He'd been living and working as a writer in a tiny set of rooms overtop a pawn shop. They'd been together ever since that night.

Though she knew everything about the man Bane had been, she knew nothing about the man he was now. He hadn't shared much of his newfound knowledge since learning of his true identity. Granted, there hadn't been a lot of time for revelations, not between all the fleeing for their lives and sex. Now he was practically a stranger to her. One she wasn't too sure she wanted to know.

CHAPTER 6

Markley's cries became more insistent. Resigned, Josie got to her feet, and as she began heading toward the cabin, Bane suddenly appeared. He'd just stepped out of the woods, and he was carrying several bags in each hand. Josie hurried over to relieve him of a couple, and together they walked to the cabin.

"Got some supplies," Bane said. "The rest is in the ship. I'll have to make a few trips to bring it all in."

"You didn't fly that ship around town, did you?"

"I'm not an idiot."

Josie ignored his tone. "I can help you carry

everything in."

They entered the cabin and put the bags on the table, then headed out the door again. Markley jumped up in the window, and Josie could hear his loud complaints about being left behind.

She laughed suddenly as they stepped into the woods. "This reminds me of that time at Christmas. Do you remember all those trips we made back and forth to that car you rented? What a great day that was."

A flicker of a smile flashed on Bane's lips. Their eyes met and held for a moment. She reached out and was a little surprised when he took her hand, bringing it to his lips. His eyes were warm. She grew hopeful as his thumb moved over her knuckles in a gentle caress. She wanted to say more, so much more, but at the same time, she was afraid to break the spell.

All too soon, the warmth in his eyes disappeared. He looked down at their hands as though they belonged to someone else. He let go and turned away.

"Let's go," he said, his voice gruff. Then he marched off.

Her steps lagged with disappointment while he strode on ahead. She watched the rigid outline of his broad shoulders for a moment and then dropped her head to concentrate on her steps.

They reached the ship, and as she took the bags he passed down to her, she was relieved to see the amount of groceries he'd bought. Her belly rumbled, reminding her she hadn't eaten since last night. It had to be just after lunch, judging by the sun shining high overhead.

Bane jumped down from the ship, and the hatch closed behind him. He then bent and picked up most of the bags.

"Is there anything else? I can carry more," she told him.

"No. That's everything." He started back the way they'd come.

She followed him, looking at the ship over her shoulder. "Don't you think we should cover it up or something? I mean, it was dark last night, so it didn't really matter, but now anyone could stumble upon it."

He kept his sights focused ahead. "Doesn't matter. At least, it won't soon."

"Why? You didn't see one of those big ships heading for town, did you?" She scanned the sky, fearful of catching a glimpse of one of the giant, menacing things floating overhead.

"No. I told you we have some time while the Cadeyrns concentrate on the big cities."

"Then what do you mean? You don't care if someone finds your ship? Isn't it on your dad's property? People may come around the cabin asking questions." His gait grew faster, and she found she had to trot to keep up with him. "Bane?"

"Let's get back, and then you'll see what I mean."

That didn't tell her anything. She let her steps falter again. Why must he always keep her in the dark? Trying to get him to open up was harder than coaxing Markley into his carrier.

They reached the cabin, and the only one not in a foul mood was the cat, who turned figure eights around both their legs. "Put this stuff away and make some lunch. I have to set something up," Bane said, then he was back out the door again, heading toward the shed.

"Aye-aye, Captain Asshole," she said under

her breath with a salute.

Josie put the groceries away and was relieved to see he'd actually thought to buy Markley his favorite food. So at least he hadn't forgotten everything about the past. When he returned, they both sat down to eat the sandwiches she'd made.

"All that other stuff. I'm not sure where you want it." Josie waved her hand at the other bags in the living room.

"Most of it can go into the shed or the spare bedroom." It was mainly staple supplies like toilet paper, paper towels, large bottles of water, batteries, and other stuff that she couldn't fit into the cupboards.

She eyed him over her sandwich. "So what'd you mean it won't matter soon if anyone sees your ship?"

He looked back over his shoulder toward the screen door. She peered past him, wondering what he was staring at. She didn't see anything.

"Soon," he answered.

"Soon what? Why does everything have to be so secretive? Can't you just tell me what the f—" Every muscle in her body froze. Her sandwich fell to the plate as she slowly stood up, stepped over the bench of the table, and moved toward the door. "What is that?"

As though in a daze, she wandered outside and went down the porch steps. A semi-transparent glass wall arched like a dome to encompass a huge area, perhaps the entire town. The screen door banged shut, alerting her to Bane's presence.

"Did you do this?" With some effort, she forced her gaze away from the sight to look at him.

"Yes, to protect the town. The Cadeyrns cannot penetrate it. We'll be safe under here."

"While the rest of the world is destroyed?"

Bane's gaze narrowed. "No, not the rest. I told you there are others like me. Each of us has infiltrated a small town and activated a shield."

So that's what those things were that he had out this morning. He was setting up this giant dome.

"But you've cut off the rest of the world. We're safe in here while out there...." She felt pressure on her arm. She stared down at his hand, then into his eyes. Distractedly, she wondered if she appeared ready to faint and his grip was merely precautionary. Her body felt numb, just as it had when she'd spotted the first UFO outside the window of her office building.

"We have to think now in terms of preservation. Not just people, but lakes, resources, animals." His tone was gentler, persuasive.

"Like an ark?"

He nodded. "You can think of it that way, yes."

Another thought entered her mind. "You said they could mess with the weather."

"Rain, sunlight, and oxygen can penetrate the shield lining. It acts like a filter, though, not allowing in too much moisture, and it won't let in anything toxic."

"How long do we stay under here?" She'd read Stephen King's *Under the Dome,* and she knew all too well how being trapped under one of these things could escalate into dangerous scenarios.

"Until it's safe to come out. Or if help arrives."

That made her hopeful. "Have you made contact with your planet somehow? Do you think they'll come?"

"No, I haven't contacted them. I can't. I'm hoping that when we Sentinels switched on, it triggered some kind of SOS signal to them. We'll have to wait and see. I have to go into town again."

"What? Why? People will be freaking out. It's not safe." Now it was her turn to grasp his arm.

"That's exactly why I need to go. I have to explain what's happening. Let them know the town is safe."

She had a bad feeling about this. "What makes you think they'll listen to you? They don't even know you. You're a stranger."

He moved back from her. "I'll tell them about the Sentinels and Gannon. And about the Cadeyrns from Centeris."

"They won't believe you. They'll think you're insane," Josie insisted.

He smiled coldly. "Not when I land my ship in the center of town." He strode toward the woods, leaving her standing there alone.

* * * *

Bane could hear Josie's steps coming up behind him, causing him to smirk. He'd suspected she wouldn't let him go into town alone. He knew what she'd be thinking. *God only knows what the people will do to him. They're already on high alert and looking for answers. No doubt they won't be too polite in asking him either.* Her presence may help alleviate the panic and suspicion that was sure to come.

"Bane, wait," she called.

He slowed his pace and turned around. "Glad you decided to join me."

She fell into step beside him. "Do you really think they'll listen to you?"

"It may take some convincing, but they'll soon come to accept what's happening is in their best interests."

She huffed. "Either that or they'll tear us both apart."

"I won't let that happen," he assured her.

Once they were on the ship, he didn't bother to conceal his flight path. Instead, he put on a bit of a show, zooming up to the top of the shield, maneuvering around the perimeter, and darting back and forth over the town, making sure as many people as possible saw him. From the corner of his eye, he spotted Josie's hands in a death grip on the armrests of her seat.

"Relax," he told her.

She glared at him. "Easy for you to say."

He loved the feel of the power of the ship.

If he'd wanted to, he could have flown right out of Earth's atmosphere and deep into outer space. He absently wondered if, like him, the other Sentinels were basking in their newfound identities and, perhaps, having activated their own shields, longed for their freedom. The technical knowledge and abilities he now possessed intrigued and delighted him.

Deep down, he'd always felt there was something different about him. He supposed that maybe everyone felt like that sometimes. In the novels he used to write, the heroes were always strong and powerful, radiating with purpose, fulfilling their destinies and saving lives, if not entire worlds. And now, wasn't he doing just that? Perhaps he'd always suspected that something else—someone else—slumbered deep within him, longing to awaken.

He would do what it took to keep the town safe, to ensure the survival of the human race. And hopefully, it would be, as he had said to Josie, that Gannon would know of Earth's fate and come to the rescue. Then he wouldn't be alone. Not that he couldn't handle the daunting task; he'd been created to play this role. And yet part of him longed for his people.

"There's the spot. We're going down, so prepare yourself," he said.

A park set in the center of town was his destination. Already a large group was gathering there. He could see them pointing up at the ship and nattering at each other speculatively. As he paused in flight to lower straight down, he watched for signs of aggression. Police were keeping the crowd under control, gesturing with their hands for people to move back from the area. They appeared to be the only ones armed. Soon the ship hovered only a few feet from the ground. He gazed at Josie and saw she sat forward in her seat, staring intently at the group.

"I think it's best if I go out first," he told her, getting to his feet. "Just in case there's any trouble."

She tugged at her seatbelt irritably, her hands shaking. As he moved to the belly of the ship and was about to open the hatch, she came up beside him. "I think we should present a united front."

He had to admit she had courage. Seeing the determination in her eyes, he nodded in agreement. "I'll go down first. Come out behind me and stay close to the ship."

"All right."

The hatch swished up, and he jumped the couple of feet to the ground. Moving forward, he heard Josie jump down behind him. The crowd had shifted back a distance from the ship, and he noted the half dozen police officers standing before them, using their outstretched arms as barriers. In the background, sirens sounded, and he caught sight of the flashing lights of more police cars and even an ambulance and a fire truck. No doubt the shield had freaked them out, and his arrival only added to the chaos. Seeing he had everyone's attention, he spread his hands wide to show he was unarmed.

"Do not be alarmed," he began. "My presence here is not to cause harm but to ensure your safety."

He paused and gauged their reaction. Most were fidgeting, trying to get a good look at him and the ship.

"I, like all of you, have spent my life on Earth, although I am not technically from your planet. There are others like me who have lived here among you, preparing for this event. We knew one day, invaders would come. That is why we are here, to protect the Earth and its people."

"Then why have you sealed us up in here like prisoners?" demanded someone from the crowd.

"The shield's purpose is to ensure your survival," Bane answered. "It will keep the invaders out."

"What's with the spaceship?" someone else demanded.

"The ships have remained dormant until the time arrived that my people were needed," Bane answered patiently. "We are Acacians, and my ancestors are from a planet far from here named Gannon. Those of us who are here are known as Sentinels—guardians of Earth."

"Have you contacted your planet to let them know we're under attack?" an older woman called out. This started some rumblings in the group. Bane heard them arguing and speculating among themselves.

"How do we know we can trust them?"

"They may be just as bad as the others."

"How do we know *they're* not *with* the others?"

"If they're here to help, why aren't they doing

anything?"

"They have. They've sealed us up to suffocate in here."

Bane spoke, raising his voice to be heard among the crowd. "My kind has walked the Earth side by side with humans since the beginning. Our objective has always been to protect humans and the planet. I have not contacted Gannon. I have no way to do so. I am assuming when the attack began, Gannon was alerted, and a force is on its way to help. In the meantime, we Sentinels have shielded as many small towns as we are able to with the goal of preservation."

A man dressed in slacks and a blue dress shirt moved forward past the police barrier. Bane noted his attire and figured he must be some sort of spokesman for the people. He also noted the man wore no tie or jacket, the top buttons of his dress shirt had been unbuttoned, and his sleeves were rolled up. He appeared exhausted and wary.

"My name is Jack Herald. I'm the mayor of this town. May we know your name and the name of your companion?"

"I'm Bane, and this is Josie."

"Is she an alien too?" a childlike voice called out from the crowd.

"No," Bane replied.

"Is she your captive?" a man asked.

Bane was becoming impatient. "No, she is here of her own free will."

He took a deep breath, calming himself. From the looks of things, this was going to be a long, tedious interview.

CHAPTER 7

The anxious look of the crowd made Josie uneasy. She feared it was only a matter of time before Bane lost patience, and his arrogance and irritation crept out. He had a huge obligation, and she knew he took his position seriously, but he was reluctant to justify his actions to those he viewed as vastly inferior. They fired question after question at him. He did his best to alleviate the crowd's fear, yet instead of reassuring them, he seemed to have the opposite effect.

"I have family outside this town. I need to get out, and I bet I'm not the only one. You need to bring this thing down and let us get to our families," a young man said.

Bane glared at him. "Let me make this perfectly clear. The shield is here for your protection. Right now, the invaders are concentrating on the larger cities. Once they're done there, they'll move on to the smaller towns. Make no mistake, what is happening outside the shields is no battle. It's an extermination. Therefore, no one leaves. No one gets in. The shield is not a revolving door. It is here to stay, no exceptions."

"We're not prisoners. Who are you to make these decisions for us?" the young man fired back. Many in the crowd voiced their agreement and outrage.

Josie saw Bane's fists clench. She knew she had to say something. She stepped up beside him to present a united front. "I know you're all concerned, but please understand what Bane says is true. We journeyed here by foot from a large city where one of those ships is hovering. The invaders are capable of manipulating the weather. They caused the blackout and the earthquakes without even leaving their ships. Right now, they're probably descending to the ground. Bane said it will be no battle, and he's right. We are dealing with vastly superior technology, and we don't stand a chance. The only option is to pray for whoever is outside of the shields and hope that help arrives soon." She looked at Bane and saw that he appeared satisfied with her words.

"So we're just supposed to sit tight and pray for help? How do we know you're even telling the truth? We've seen nothing here, apart from the initial arrival of the ships on the news. We're cut off from the media due to the power outage, but there's no proof the invaders caused it. Yes, there have been some storms and quakes, but that's not considered unusual. How do we know the invaders are here to destroy us? For that matter, how do we know if they're even still out there anymore? We have your word, and that's all. Maybe you've sealed us up in here like some science experiment, keeping us from escaping. Maybe he's the enemy," a middle-aged woman accused, pointing a defiant finger at Bane.

Bane shook his head. He held up his hands when the crowd began to badger him again. "You have to trust what we're saying is the truth. I can assure you those ships are still out there, and their sole intent is to rape this planet for its resources and to obliterate humanity. It's what they do. Things are going to get a lot worse."

"I don't give a shit what you say. Bring this thing down and let those of us who want to leave, leave. I, for one, am willing to take my chances out there. It sure as hell is better than hiding in here like a coward."

"Yeah!" agreed several of them. Many glared and pointed at Bane, screaming, "Coward!"

The mayor raised his hands, vainly begging for patience.

"Insolent, ungrateful, ignorant fools," Bane suddenly bellowed.

The people quieted and stared at him in shock.

"Bane, stop it!" Josie cried.

She saw the angry young man break free of the barrier and reach into his jacket for what she feared was a weapon. She pointed and screamed as he pulled out a gun. Lightning fast, Bane responded. He pushed her to the ground. She looked up in time to see him pull a palm-sized, shiny ring from his back pants pocket. The man waved his gun around, yelling for the police to get back as they drew their weapons. Bane held the ring at arm's length, lining it up with the threat. The sun glinted off the ring, and suddenly a beam of light shot out of the center of it toward the crowd. The light widened and encompassed the gunman along with several others, including all of the police officers. They immediately tensed up and shook as though electrocuted. The beam of light held them captive in its glow. As the light died away, everyone caught within its range collapsed to the ground.

Several people screamed. Anyone able to move scattered. The only person holding a weapon now that Josie could detect was Bane. She leapt to her feet and grabbed hold of his arm. "Are they dead? Did you kill them?"

He shook her off, staring impassively out at the crowd. "They're debilitated, but they'll live."

The mayor was the only one who held his ground. He came forward until he was several feet from them. "Is this how you plan to protect this town? With threats and violence?" he demanded. Josie was impressed with his bravado.

"You saw what happened. I was forced to protect myself," Bane said. He turned to Josie, no doubt expecting her to back him up, but she was no longer paying attention to the exchange going on before her. Her gaze was riveted up over their heads toward the sky.

"It's happening again," she said.

Massive, black clouds gathered overhead. The light inside the shield grew dimmer and dimmer as the sun was slowly overshadowed. She swept her gaze around the park and noticed that the crowd, who had rapidly dispersed, now slowed their steps, turning their heads upward. The stunned men on the ground shook their heads groggily and got to their feet as though rising from a long slumber. They, too, looked upward.

Suddenly, Josie felt a rumble beneath her feet. Just as a bolt of lightning flashed and ricocheted off the shield with a loud *crack*, the ground gave a violent shake. Many people lost their balance and fell to their knees. Bane's hand shot out and grabbed hold of her arm before she stumbled. All those who had fled from Bane now rushed back toward him.

"What's happening?" a young woman cried. "Are we under attack?"

The ground heaved again. The crowd struggled for balance and fell into one other while grabbing at bodies close to them. A tree shuddered and fell to the ground close by. Several birds cried out and flew around in disarray. The swings on the playground swayed back and forth. People cried, and some prayed aloud.

"Prepare yourself," Bane said the words close to her ear.

She looked up at him in shock. "For what? What's happening? You said we'd be safe in here."

"We will be."

The ground lurched as though someone had yanked it upward. If not for Bane's grip on her, she would have fallen as others around them toppled.

"Save us," some cried, arms outstretched toward Bane.

Despite the dim light, rapid bursts of lightning allowed the outline of the shield to be clearly visible since it was only several blocks away. The land beyond the shield was also visible, although it now appeared to be out of sync with the land within. Strangely, Josie's line of sight became disoriented. She blinked hard several times, certain she wasn't seeing correctly. As bizarre as it seemed, the shield appeared to be lifting up and taking the town with it.

"The shield will protect you," Bane yelled,

remaining calm while chaos reigned all around him.

Lightning continued to pummel the shield, and each time it was reflected away in a riot of sparks and cracking sounds. Higher and higher, the shield lifted them. People remained on their knees or tried to make their way across the open grass. Within the shield, the ground no longer shook, yet the force of being lifted made the ground unsteady to walk upon.

"What's happening?" someone cried.

"Bane, are we lifting up?" Josie demanded, grasping at his shirt for leverage.

He put his arm around her waist and held her close. "Yes, we're lifting up. The shield is responding to the earthquakes and is protecting us. Once we've reached a safe enough distance, it will stop."

"How high above the ground will we go?" Josie asked in wonder.

"About a hundred feet or so. From where we are, it'll appear much higher."

"I don't understand how this is happening. How can a dome be lifting us up? What's supporting the ground beneath us?" Josie demanded.

Bane smiled. "You're thinking of the shield as a dome. Think of it more as one of those snow globes. You know, the kind you see in the stores at Christmas time? The ones you shake upside down to make the snow fall?"

Josie nodded.

"A huge chunk of the Earth has lifted up beneath us, ensuring entire lakes, underground springs, and resources all are intact. It's what we call an orb-shield."

How incredible. Josie understood perfectly now. It wasn't a dome at all. It was so much more.

* * * *

It was almost fully dark when Bane and Josie arrived back at the cabin. Bane landed his spaceship right in the driveway; there was no need to hide it from sight any longer. The bubble, or orb-shield as Bane had called it, had stopped lifting several minutes after it began, and the ground beneath their feet had become stable. People had flocked toward him after that, crying out for answers. Now that they were no longer displaying hostility, Bane had magnanimously answered all questions put to him.

Patiently, he'd explained that the orb-shield was self-activating, sensing when danger was imminent and acting accordingly to protect those enclosed within. Dark storm clouds above had continued to display their wrath, and Albion's mayor had asked what was to protect them from the relentless downpour. Bane had gone on to explain the shield's abilities. It allowed in sunlight, oxygen, and rain. But the permeable shell acted as a filter, not allowing in too much moisture, harmful rays, or anything other than safe, unpolluted, breathable air—just in case the Cadeyrns attempted to poison or suffocate those within. Bane had reassured everyone that the town would be safe floating in the sky away from any earthquakes, floods, or fires, which relieved Josie and the others, but at the same time, made them bow their heads in fear for others outside the safety of the shield.

Markley was thrilled when they entered the cabin. Josie bent to scoop him up into her arms. She'd been so afraid when the crowd had grown hostile and turned on Bane. And seeing that man with the gun had filled her with a terror she could hardly comprehend. In that moment, she'd faced the possibility of Bane's destruction. No matter how he was now, she still couldn't imagine her life without him. It was true he'd become hard and cold, not just to her but to mankind itself, but he used that detachment to do what needed to be done. He'd saved them. Not just her and Markley but the town of Albion as well.

Bane went back outside, saying that he had to check on things in the shed, and when he returned, Josie was preparing their dinner.

"Tomorrow, I'll meet with the mayor to begin setting up the town's power supply. I don't have enough energy to set up every household, but supermarkets, some stores, the hospital, the fire department, the police station, and all the important places will be hooked up. I asked Jack to make a list of priority locations."

Josie had seen the two of them with their heads together in deep discussion after the orb had stopped moving. She had a feeling Bane was humoring the mayor, giving him tasks and the impression they were a team, whereas she knew Bane was the one in charge and calling the shots. She pitied anyone who thought otherwise.

They ate dinner in relative silence. She had a

lot on her mind, and she could tell by the calculating look on Bane's face that he was already planning his next three moves. She wondered what other surprises he might have in store for Albion.

She watched him speculatively over the course of the meal, wishing for some sign that he'd revert back to his former self now that the town was safe, though the detached look on his face remained.

"How long do you think we'll have to be up in the air like this?" she asked, breaking the silence.

"Depends. We're safer up here anyhow, and I won't have to listen to people in town complaining to get out or to let others in. It's bad enough hearing the list of demands from the mayor."

She didn't know if she could bear the thought of people trapped outside the dome, pounding desperately to get in. Up here, they wouldn't be subjected to that. It was a cold and merciless thought, but perhaps he was right? She forced the image from her mind.

"Why do you have a spaceship? Is it in case the shield didn't work and you had to battle the enemy? Or is it to convince the town that you're actually who you say you are? I mean, a spaceship is a pretty convincing evidence that you're not from Earth." They'd used the ship to get to town faster, but considering how far they'd had to walk to reach it, she figured the purpose of it was not exactly for travel.

"Yes, it's for the things you mentioned, but it also allows me to leave here once the town is secure."

"Leave? But aren't you supposed to stay and oversee the town's defense? Why do you have to leave? Where are you going?" She didn't want him to leave. Or did he plan to take her with him?

The look on his face made her feel like a nagging wife. "I'm leaving to battle the Cadeyrns. The shield will see to your safety."

So he obviously didn't intend to take her with him. He apparently didn't have any qualms about leaving her either. Seeing the determined look on his face, she knew better than to question his decision. Resigned and annoyed with always finding out his plans way after the fact, she asked, "When do you leave?"

"Tomorrow after the power is set up in town. I'm meeting with the mayor as well. I told him to gather the heads of emergency services so we can discuss the safety of the town. I told him the shield will stay in place and doesn't need me here to oversee it."

"How long will you be gone?"

He shrugged. "As long as it takes."

So he planned to go out there and face the Cadeyrns in battle, to put his life on the line for the sake of humanity. She felt sick with dread. "But how are you going to get out? You said the shield is impenetrable. Are you going to take it down to fly out?" He'd have to lower them to the ground first, obviously.

His tight smile appeared to patronize her. "There's a device onboard my ship that allows me to pass through the shield without causing any damage."

"What if the Cadeyrns possess that ability as well?"

"They don't."

She couldn't believe he was going to leave her there while he went off into battle. "What if something happens to you?"

"Like I said, the shield will protect you as

long as it's needed. If the threat to the town ends, the orb will lower back into place, and the shield will come down."

"But what about me? What about us?" She wanted to grab hold of him and shake that blank look off his face. He had finished his dinner and pushed his plate aside. As he got to his feet, she could see he was becoming irritated.

"You'll be safe as well."

She stood up. "But you might not be. You've never been in battle before. You're a writer, for God's sake!"

"And now I'm a Sentinel. I assure you, necessary skills have been hardwired into my being." He seemed annoyed that she'd dared to remind him of his earlier existence. "Why don't you go to bed? You look tired." He walked past her and went out the door, his heavy steps pounding down the stairs.

After staring long and hard at his back, she picked up the cat and went to bed.

The next morning when she got up, Bane was already gone. He'd taken his ship, and she had a gut feeling he wasn't coming back to say goodbye before he left. Annoyed, she fed the cat, got dressed, and put on her hiking boots, determined to walk into town. If she followed the dirt road to the main road, she could probably make it in an hour or so. Even though Bane was being an asshole, she was determined he wasn't going to leave her without a proper goodbye.

CHAPTER 8

Bane was coming out of the police station when Josie finally spotted him. She'd noted on her trek through town that some of the stores had signs in the windows announcing they now had power. That was fast.

"Bane," she called out, increasing her pace to match his swift strides. Wherever he was going, he was in a hurry. Hearing his name, he stopped and glanced around. Josie waved and went over to him. "Are you leaving now?"

He smirked. "In a hurry to get rid of me?"

She couldn't tell if he was joking or not. They stood on the sidewalk in front of Albion's library. Bane hadn't bothered to connect the power in there, she noted, as it was still locked up tight with a closed sign on the door. A number of people were on the street, most of them carrying bags, anxious to stock up on supplies now that some shops were open for business. The inevitable stares and guarded looks were directed their way.

"I was afraid I'd miss you before you left," she said.

"You would have. I'm leaving now."

She bristled at his callous tone. "Can I walk with you to the ship?"

He shrugged and turned to walk away. "Suit yourself."

She fell into step behind him. He'd parked his ship in a clearing surrounded by tall trees. He took a remote from his pocket and opened the hatch without slowing his pace. Josie reached out and grabbed hold of his hand. "Wait! Aren't you even going to kiss me goodbye?"

He exhaled in a huff. Stiffly, he bent his head and kissed her hard on the lips. As he went to move away, she grabbed hold of his jacket and pulled him close again. Entangling her fingers in his collar, she held him captive and went up on her tiptoes to kiss him. Despite the coldness of his lips, she felt him slowly relax. Heat washed over her as his tongue darted into her mouth. Greedy hands began pawing at her breasts before moving down to cup her ass, lifting her up against his arousal.

"I want you before I leave," he said, his breath hot against her neck.

She nodded her head in agreement. Oblivious to their precarious surroundings, he undid her pants and pushed them down around her knees. She felt the cool air against her skin and self-consciously peered around. Bane undid his pants and pulled them down enough to free his erection. Swiftly, before he lost interest, she bent to untie her bootlaces and kick off her jeans and panties. He moved his hands to her ass and lifted her into position so her legs wrapped around his hips. Lowering her, he eased inside her and backed up to brace himself against the spaceship. His strokes were swift and intense, deep and unforgiving. She lost herself in ecstasy while he took her masterfully without reserve.

Her climax came fast and hard, overwhelming her and making her cry out, "I love you, I love you!"

His grip on her ass tightened. He stiffened

and came hard, gasping and grunting his release. Moments later, he lowered her and tugged his pants back into place. She felt saddened by his refusal to offer her the slightest endearment, considering they were parting for what might be forever.

She dressed with haste. "Be careful. Don't take any chances. I love you, Bane. Come back to me."

His cool expression faltered momentarily. He reached out and tucked a stray curl behind her ear. "I'll do what has to be done. If I die completing my mission, so be it. Goodbye." He nodded his head in her direction and turned to leap up into the open door of the ship.

He stood facing her as the hatch swished down, blocking him from view. A few minutes later, the ship lifted up and was gone. She lost sight of it briefly as it disappeared high into the sky. The sun glinted off the top and sides of the orb, and she spotted the ship as it approached the barrier.

A ray of light shot forth from the ship. It appeared to penetrate the translucent wall, but then she saw that the shield had changed to a dark blue where the ray of light hit. Slowly, the vessel eased forward. She held her breath as it slipped easily through the small circle of blue. Once the ship was outside of the shield, the bluish color quickly faded away as though it had never been. A few seconds later, the ship shot off and was gone from sight.

Josie sat down on the grass and began to cry. As her sobs subsided, she heard what sounded like someone clearing their throat. She got to her feet. "Is someone there?"

The man who'd pulled the gun at the park had appeared. His hands were raised, displaying he was unarmed, and he wore a bashful look on his face. "I'm not packing, I swear."

She took an involuntary step back. "What do you want?"

He didn't move any closer, only swept his gaze around the area as though searching for something. "I'd say I didn't mean to interrupt, but it looks like you're alone. I would have sworn I heard something."

Yeah, me and Bane having sex, she thought with embarrassment. "I wasn't alone." She looked up into the sky.

The man followed her gaze and then nodded

in understanding. "Ah, he took off."

"Yes."

He smiled. "So I wasn't hearing things."

Despite what had happened yesterday, she felt her defenses lift slightly. Everyone had been terrified at the park, and she could understand how things had gotten out of hand. She smiled back at the young man. "No, you weren't."

Encouraged, he moved toward her and stretched out his hand. "I'm Vincent. My friends call me Vince."

"Okay...." She trailed off, not sure how to address him.

He laughed. "Or, in your case, you can call me Neurotic Jerk."

Now she laughed. "Everyone was pretty tense," she admitted.

He looked at her without a trace of humor. "I wouldn't have shot anyone. The gun wasn't even loaded. I'm sorry if I freaked you out."

"In view of the circumstances, I can understand your reaction. We were all pretty freaked out, I think."

"Yeah, but not everyone was pulling out

weapons." He laughed again. "He got me good, though. Serves me right for pulling a gun on an alien…or what was that he called himself?"

"A Sentinel."

"Yes, a Sentinel, an imposing title. Although, I guess it should be, seeing as how they're here to, you know, save the world and all."

She would have taken offense if he'd sounded sarcastic, but he hadn't.

He gestured upward. "So where's he off to?"

She wasn't sure if she should reveal Bane's plans or not, but considering he'd already told the leaders of Albion that he'd be leaving, she figured it'd be a matter of public knowledge soon enough.

"Now that the town is secure, Bane left to battle the invaders." She felt a little shiver run through her at the thought. He was actually gone, and she didn't know if she would ever see him again. A stray tear slipped down her cheek, and she rubbed at it absently.

Vincent stared at her with confusion. "He left? But how'd he get out? I mean, that's what our huge beef was yesterday—not leaving once the shield was in place. He said no one leaves, and no one gets in."

"He must have meant only the townspeople. He obviously didn't mean himself since he planned to leave all along once we were safe. Although, I just found out about it last night." She couldn't keep the bitterness from her voice. "His ship has special technology allowing it to penetrate the shield without bringing it down or undermining it. I saw him go. He passed right through it."

"Wow. Impressive." Vincent stared up at the sky, then dropped his gaze to hers once more. "That must have been a bit of a shock to you—him springing it on you that he was leaving."

Josie nodded once. "I understand. I mean, he's so focused right now on keeping everyone safe."

Vincent looked at her with compassion. "Of course. The pressure he's under must be considerable. But still…."

If he kept looking at her that way, she was afraid she'd break down again. "I should get going. It's a long walk back." She headed toward the trees, and Vincent fell into step beside her.

"You're staying out at that cabin in the middle of nowhere on Bentley Lake, right?" The look she gave him obviously portrayed her confusion. "It's what a bunch of us in town thought since it's so secluded and all. It's the perfect place to hide out," he explained.

Josie figured there was no harm in him knowing where she was staying. "Yes, I am."

"Hey, my truck is just across the street in the lot. Would you like me to give you a lift? I'm actually a nice guy, I'll have you know."

She laughed. "Oh, you are, are you?" She'd heard about residents in small towns being so neighborly, and she knew she needed to make an attempt to fit in. Who knew how long they were all going to be stuck inside the orb together?

He laughed as well. "I can't have you running off thinking I'm an asshole."

"I didn't…."

He placed his hand over his heart as though wounded. "Oh, you did! All this time, you were being polite, but really you were thinking—"

"No, I wasn't, really." She knew he was teasing her, but it felt good to laugh again. "All right, I accept your offer."

Together they left the shelter of the trees and

crossed the street to his truck.

Josie invited Vince—as he insisted she call him—in for lunch. He hadn't given off any crazy vibes along the drive home, and she found herself enjoying his sense of humor and the way he poked fun at himself. They soon sat on the back deck, eating sandwiches and drinking cola. She admitted to herself he reminded her of Bane. Not Sentinel Bane, but old Bane, the one she'd fallen head over heels for. Markley sat in the bedroom window behind her, and she could hear his tail thrashing back and forth.

"He knows I'm allergic to him, and he wants to get his claws into me," Vince said, indicating the cat. As soon as they'd walked in, the cat had hissed loudly at the intruder. Josie, noting Markley's murderous look, had suggested Vince head out onto the front deck.

"He's upset his daddy's gone." Although Bane hadn't acted overly fond of Markley the past several days either.

"His daddy? Oh, that's cute."

The expression on his face made her laugh. "There's been so many changes for him. I'm surprised he's handled it all so well." She meant Markley.

Vince set his empty plate down and rubbed the crumbs off his hands. "There have been a lot of changes for the entire world. I'm surprised we're all not waving guns around."

She was thoughtful for a moment. "I think that's why the Sentinels concentrate on the smaller towns—a lot fewer people to worry about. They seem more laid-back here and not as prone to the hysteria you'd see in the big cities with a mass population." She'd seen firsthand the effect the invaders had on her city. She could only imagine how insane it was there now.

When Vince didn't respond to her ponderings and remained silent and thoughtful, she asked him what was wrong.

"Oh, nothing. I just find my mind wandering to all kinds of dark places sometimes."

"Are you worried? Bane assured me we'd be safe here."

He didn't appear convinced. "I know, but don't you ever question what he tells you? From what you've said, I get the impression he's not the same man you knew."

"He's not. He's completely different," she admitted.

"Different, how?"

She shrugged, not really wanting to talk about her concerns, yet at the same time, relieved to have someone to confide in. "He's completely focused on his mission. It's a huge weight to carry and probably the reason why he's been so commando, so cold."

"I know I shouldn't mention this, but yesterday in the park, the way he spoke to us—*at* us—I got the impression he didn't even want to be here. As though he resented having to protect us. But it's probably, as you said, he's carrying a huge weight."

Josie didn't want to admit that Vince was right. She'd felt an underlying resentment, almost distaste in Bane, not just for her but for all humans. Maybe it was stress, or maybe it was because the Acacians were so vastly superior. Who knew?

"You must be worried about him. I'm sure he'll be fine, though. Probably be back before you know it." He attempted to change the subject, obviously seeing her unease. He got to his feet. "I should go."

Josie didn't really want to be left alone, but she could think of no legitimate reason to keep Vince there. "It was nice talking to you."

He nodded and smiled, moved toward the stairs, then paused. "If you like, I could pick you up tomorrow, and we could go to Eagle's View. It's that big hill in town. There's a road you can drive up right to the top, and there's a lookout. It'll give you a chance to see all of Albion."

"I'd like that," she said.

"Okay. Pick you up around ten?" When Josie nodded in agreement, he started to descend the steps but paused again. "I'm sorry about what I said with Bane not liking us. We *are* a pretty annoying race." He laughed. "There's no reason for him to dislike us. Unless he's actually the enemy…. Sorry. There goes my maniacal mind again. That'd be pretty crazy, don't you think? I mean, we're completely trapped in here. Who's to say one of those big UFOs won't come along and attach a tractor beam and haul us across the universe?" He laughed again. "Can you tell I watch a lot of *Star Trek*? I'll see you tomorrow."

Josie went over to lean against the railing of the deck. Vince was only joking around, but what he said made her suddenly anxious. What if he was just repeating what others had said in town? And the worst thing of all…what if it was true?

It was not an idea she'd ever entertained; that Bane could be the enemy. But what if he were? It would make perfect sense, actually. The way he seemed to despise humans and how he'd conveniently penned them up in here and then gone off to God knew where. Sure, he'd said he was going to fight the Cadeyrns, but what if that was a lie? What if everything he said was a lie?

When the UFOs showed up and all those Sentinels—if that's what they really were—turned on, maybe they were the ground force tasked with securing as many human specimens as possible? Like that old television series *V*, they could be preserving people in the small towns for a victory party snack. Not to mention the amount of freshwater lakes Bane had handily sealed up in this bubble as well.

She squeezed the rail beneath her hands and told herself to get a grip. There was no way Bane was the enemy. Vince had stirred up her imagination, but that was all it was—a fantasy. Bane was no more a danger to this town than she was.

* * * *

Bane decided to fly over the town before heading to the cabin. The past four days had been extremely long and difficult. Returning to the city he and Josie had fled, he'd witnessed complete devastation.

As he'd feared, the Cadeyrns had come down from their ships, eliminating as many people as possible. As he'd told Josie, the weapons they used disintegrated up to ten people in one shot, leaving no trace of slaughter. Yet, the city was in an uproar, and the carnage from trampled bodies or those hurt or killed from flying or crumbling debris was in no short supply. Most windows had blown out from the earthquakes. If buildings stood at all, glass, metal, and hazardous rubble lay strewn all around streets, blocking alleyways and sidewalks, making travel difficult and dangerous.

He'd flown over a mass exodus of people fleeing for their lives, many carrying nothing more than children or their pets in their arms and the clothes on their backs. Using all the weapons at his disposal, he'd fired upon the enemy whenever and wherever able, to no or little effect. He'd inflicted damage, but there were just too damn many of them. This morning he'd given up, knowing he could make but a dent in the enemies' armor, and prayed that backup would soon arrive.

Fueled by only a few hours of sleep snatched here and there the past few days, he reentered the orb with relief, knowing that a meal and bed awaited him. And Josie.

Seeing the apartment building they'd lived in together standing mercifully erect among scattered slabs of steel and concrete reminded him of the life they'd shared together. They, like this building, had withstood the destruction. But for how long? Vestiges of their romance had crept into his uneasy slumber when his defenses had been low, leaving him with warm, nostalgic feelings upon rising. It amazed him how much he longed to see her face again.

The town was on the verge of dusk and eerily calm and quiet. He brought his ship down before the cabin and leapt from the open hatch to jog toward the deck.

"Jose?" he called, bursting through the door.

Markley cried out and practically leapt into his arms from the table. Bane stroked his sleek fur and talked to him gently while he moved through the cabin. Josie wasn't inside, and when he saw that Markley's food and water bowl were empty, he grew concerned. He filled up both bowls and watched as the cat lapped greedily at the water before turning to the food. It appeared he'd gone some time without either.

Bane left the cabin, and after checking that the canoe was still flipped over at the water's edge, he jumped back into his ship and raced for town.

CHAPTER 9

Josie clung to the bars of the cell inside Albion's police station. For two days, she'd remained a prisoner. Worried for Markley, she'd begged one of the officers to go out to the cabin and feed her cat. God only knew if he'd actually done it or not.

The day after Bane left, the town started to turn on him. It began with slight doubts and speculations, but by the second day, things had snowballed out of control. Vince had taken her to visit Eagle's View as promised, and the outing had been pleasant enough. The next day she learned that after taking her home, he'd gone right to the police station, spreading rumors and propaganda against Bane. It hadn't taken much to make the small, suspicious town believe all that he said.

The following afternoon she'd been lured to town with a promise of a picnic in the park, but instead, she'd been brought before a mob in the very place where Bane had assured everyone of their safety. Unable to answer their outrageous, accusing questions, she'd been taken away to use as security in the event of Bane's return. Fearful of his technology, the people had figured she was the only bargaining chip they possessed.

Just as she sat down on her cot to rest for the night, she heard all hell break loose. Inside her cell, she could see nothing, but she heard an explosion and several alarms going off in rapid succession. Shouting soon followed. She made out Bane's voice and could tell he was getting closer to her. Soon she heard him calling her name.

"Bane, I'm in here," she cried.

Moments later, he was in the room, standing before the bars. Several armed police and even some townsfolk cradling shotguns surrounded him. He seemed not to notice or care. He reached through the bars and took hold of her hands.

"Are you all right? Did they hurt you? I swear

to God if they hurt you…."

Josie had never seen him so enraged. "No, I'm okay. I'm just worried about Markley," Her voice caught on a sob. "Why are you doing this to us?" she aimed that question at Jack Herald, the mayor, who'd stepped into the room.

"Everyone needs to settle down," Jack said. "There's no need for guns or violence."

"The hell there isn't," snapped Vince, stepping forward.

Bane spun around and grabbed him by the throat so fast that no one had time to react. Slowly, he picked Vince up off the floor until they were at eye level. "Open this up, or he dies," Bane said with a snarl.

At once, it sounded like a hundred guns were cocked.

"Bane, put him down, please," Josie begged.

Vince's face turned pitch red, and he struggled for every breath.

Suddenly a gun leveled on her.

"Drop him or she dies," the police chief stated furiously.

Bane immediately let go of Vince, who

collapsed to the floor.

"Now, here's what's going to happen," the chief said. "We're going to unlock that door and let your girlfriend out, and you're going to get in there instead."

"No!" cried Josie.

"Fine," Bane agreed. The cell door was opened, and as Josie passed Bane, he pulled her into his arms briefly. "Don't worry," he said.

Bane was locked in the cell and ordered to disarm while a gun was held on Josie. He complied and handed over various weapons tucked in his boots, belt, and strapped to his arms and legs, along with his small, circular weapon that had zapped the group in the park.

Confident that he posed no more threat, the mayor urged most of the men to clear the room.

Josie clung to Bane through the bars. "I'm so sorry."

"It's not your fault," he told her. He turned his icy stare on the police chief and Jack. "What's going on? I leave for a few days, and the whole town goes to hell."

"Hold on there, son," Jack said, holding up a

hand. "We've got some concerns."

Vince shook his head and climbed wearily to his feet. "Son of a bitch."

"Be glad you're on that side," Bane sneered at him.

"See, I warned you how dangerous he is. Here to save humanity, my ass," Vince swore.

"You're wrong about him, *Vincent*," Josie spat.

Jack turned to her. "Why don't you head on home and let us work this out?"

"I'm not leaving," Josie argued.

"Yes, you are," Bane confirmed. "I need you to be safe, Jose. Go back to the cabin, okay? Markley needs you."

The gentleness of his voice made her tear up again. Numbly, she nodded her head. "I'll be back first thing in the morning. He'd better be free by then, or there will be hell to pay."

"Are you threatening an officer of the law, ma'am?" one of the remaining officers asked.

"Damn right, I am."

"No, she's not. She's leaving," Bane assured them. "Jose, go. Let me handle this."

She nodded, not trusting herself to speak, and backed from the room. Once outside, she stood on the sidewalk for several minutes. Resigned, she trekked through town and passed by the park. A crowd had gathered around Bane's ship, which sat defiantly in the center of the field. Several minutes later, as she walked down the dark road to the cabin, the bright glow of headlights came up behind her.

Vince pulled up beside her in his truck and leaned out the window. "Want a ride?"

"Go fuck yourself."

He kept rolling along beside her as she quickened her pace. "Come on now. Don't be like that."

"All of this is your fault! No one had any doubts about Bane until you started spreading your lies. I thought you were a nice guy, but you're an asshole."

He gunned forward and pulled the truck across the road in front of her. Jumping down from the cab, he stalked toward her.

Josie backed away. "Stay away from me. I'm warning you."

"What are you gonna do? Sic your alien

boyfriend on me? Oh, that's right, he's detained at the moment."

Josie wanted to punch that smirk right off his face. She bent down and picked a palm-sized rock off the side of the road. When Vince continued forward, she drilled the rock straight at his head. Amazingly, it hit him square between the eyes and sent him stumbling to the ground.

When he didn't move, Josie approached him cautiously. As she bent down beside him, she saw a gash on his forehead. There was no blood. Curious, she knelt and touched the wound. His skin felt strange beneath her fingertips, almost rubbery. She pinched the edge of the gash and tugged slightly, only to fly back in shock when it tore away and revealed bleached, scaly skin beneath.

His hand suddenly shot up and grabbed hold of her wrist. Josie snatched the rock by his side and bashed at his face. Horrifyingly, his skin tore away to reveal a hideous form beneath. Releasing her, he grasped his head and rolled away as she continued her assault. He soon passed out and lay still on the road. Josie sprung to her feet and raced toward the truck. It was still running, and as soon as she leapt in, she put it in drive, floored the accelerator, and spun it around, heading back to town.

She came to a skidding, sideways stop before the police station and barreled inside. Two officers leapt up as she rushed past them into the room where Bane was being held.

"He's an alien," she cried, reaching for Bane's hands through the bars.

The officers, weapons drawn, burst into the room right behind her. She feared they'd pull her away, but her words must have startled them.

Bane held her as best he could. "Goddamn it! You mean that guy Vincent? I saw him rush out of here right after you left. He went after you, didn't he? Did he hurt you?"

"No, but he tried. I threw a rock at him. My God! His skin—it's not real. It covers his body, but part of it came away where I hit him. He was all white and scaly beneath."

Bane clenched his fists. "I feared something like this might happen."

"What do you mean?"

"Yeah, what do you mean?" one of the officers repeated.

"Many of the towns that should have been in orb-shields lay in ruin," he told them. "I was afraid that spies had been sent down early to infiltrate the towns and betray the Sentinels. It's one of the reasons I returned so quickly. I believed Albion was safe since we'd completed the transition, but I couldn't be sure. I had to see for myself."

"This is bullshit," one of the officers charged.

"Just go out there, the Number Nine road out of town toward the cabin. See for yourself," Josie dared him.

She breathed a sigh of relief when one of the officers left. Twenty minutes later, he returned, telling her there'd been no sign of Vincent anywhere.

* * * *

Josie slept in the police station in a chair beside Bane's cell all night. Bane's insistence that the town was in imminent danger had fallen on deaf ears.

"They don't understand what he's capable of," he'd told her. She couldn't believe she'd spent time alone with that thing.

The morning dawned clear and bright but brought with it no reprieve for Bane. Last evening everyone still insisted he was the enemy and couldn't be trusted. As to the mystery of Vincent, it remained just that—a mystery. Josie feared they suspected her of foul play, and she'd wind up in the cell beside Bane.

When one of the officers brought them coffee, she wearily got to her feet and stretched. Suddenly the floor jerked violently, causing her to fall.

"What the hell?" the officer yelled, spilling hot coffee all over his uniform.

"Damn it! Look outside," Bane hollered. "Is the orb shifting? Are we going down?"

"Hold on," the officer said as he rushed from the room.

"You said it would come down by itself when the danger passed." Josie used the bars of his cell for leverage to climb to her feet. Bane reached for her hands and held them tight.

"The danger hasn't passed. Something or some*one* is bringing down the orb," he informed her.

The floor lurched again, and Josie staggered but held tight to Bane. At the same time, the officer practically flew back into the room and fell down on his knees. "What's happening? Has the threat passed? We are definitely in descent," he informed them as he cautiously got to his feet and braced himself against the wall.

"You need to let him out of here," Josie insisted.

Bane fastened a hard gaze on the man. "You have to listen to me. That guy Vincent is what Josie said—an alien. He has tampered with my protegats and is causing the orb to reattach to the Earth. When that happens, he'll bring down the shield, and the enemy will advance on us."

The officer put a hand to his head. "Damn it! I don't know what to do."

"Listen to him!" Josie practically screamed. "Please! Or it will be the end of us all."

Confused, the man stared at both of them and then rushed from the room.

Josie headed after him. "You need to let him out! He can't help us if he's locked up."

The man flung his keys to the floor and rushed toward the door to join the other officers. He paused momentarily and stared back at her. "God help us all if you're wrong." Then he was gone.

Josie grabbed the keys and ran to free Bane.

Minutes later, they were both running through town. The ground lurched and swayed, making for a frightening dash to the park. Townspeople flooded the streets, fearful of their shaking homes. Many cried out for Bane to help them, while others cursed him for betraying them. Just as they reached the park, a giant *thunk* almost brought them to their knees. She could see from the alignment of the ground beyond the shield that the orb had embedded itself back into the Earth.

Bane skidded to a stop in front of his ship and took a moment to manually open the hatch. It whisked up, and he leapt aboard. As he put out his hand for her, a huge shadow crept across the sky. She peered up, worried the storm clouds had moved in again and the ground would begin to rumble with tremors once more. But it wasn't storm clouds.

"Shit! Bane, they're right outside the shield!" Now fully in view, a giant UFO hovered ominously.

"Hurry, Jose." Grabbing hold of her hand, Bane pulled her up into the ship and moments later, they flew off.

With fast sweeps, he spanned the town and forests, using his equipment to try and locate

Vincent. They stopped to ensure one by one that his protegats were in position.

"He hasn't tampered with them. I don't understand how he's manipulating the shield. He must be doing it another way," Bane said, running a hand over his head.

As they stood outside, Bane staring intently at the shield and the UFO hovering above, the shield suddenly disappeared.

"No!" Josie cried. "Nothing is stopping them from getting in now."

Bane took her into his arms. "I won't let them hurt you, Jose, or this town," he promised.

Josie stared up into the face of the man she loved. Unbelievably, the worst possible moment of her life was also the best. "Bane?"

He smiled down at her and bent to kiss her. His lips lingered momentarily. Taking her hand, he led her toward the ship. "I'm taking you back to the cabin. I can secure the building. That way, I know no matter what, you'll be safe."

"I want to stay with you," she insisted.

"I can't fight them if I'm worried about you."

Was she imagining it, or had her Bane actually

returned to her? Just as he was about to lift her up to the ship, a laser blast careened off the side of it. Bane spun around and pulled a concealed weapon from his belt—one that he'd neglected to turn over to the police.

"Stay still, or I'll kill her," Vincent said. He held a small metal wand in his hand and aimed it at them. "I don't want to kill her—I want her very much." His tongue flicked out to lick his lips suggestively.

Josie gasped when she saw him. More pieces of flesh on his face and chest had peeled back, revealing the ghostly white reptilian skin beneath.

"You, however, I will have no problem killing," he said to Bane before he turned his gaze to Josie. "Come with me now, and I'll let him go."

"She's not going anywhere with you," Bane informed him. In one fluid motion, he both fired his weapon at Vincent and tossed Josie through the open doorway of his ship.

She cried out as the hatch flew down to block them from view. In vain, she pounded on the door, frantic as she heard the unmistakable sounds of battle.

It seemed a lifetime later when the door finally swished up, and Bane stood there covered in slime. Vincent was nowhere to be seen, but pieces of white reptilian flesh lay scattered all over the ground.

Josie leapt into Bane's arms. "Oh, God! Is he dead?"

Bane held her tight. "He's dead."

His grip on her tightened, causing her to look toward the sky. "Bane! What is that?"

What appeared to be dozens of smaller spaceships suddenly filled the sky.

"They're descending. We need to go now!" Bane replied.

Together they leapt aboard his ship and flew off toward the cabin.

Bane brought them down to land in the driveway. He exited the ship first, his wary eyes toward the sky. Josie took his offered hand and jumped down beside him. Her gaze followed his.

"There's so many of them," she said. He would never be able to defeat them all alone.

"Go inside. I'll be right in." He strode off toward the shed.

Hearing Markley's frantic cries from the

window, Josie rushed inside. She scooped the cat into her arms. "It's all right, baby. Daddy's making the cabin safe. We'll be all right," she crooned, too terrified to think about what would happen next.

Bane joined them and wrapped them in the circle of his arms. "The cabin and the immediate area are surrounded by an invisible force field. It'll keep them out. I'm not sure for how long since they seem to have developed some new technology. It enabled Vincent to overcome the orb-shield from within, and I have no idea what else they've got up their sleeves. Everything I'm working with is ancient."

Josie heard the frustration in his voice. "You're doing the best you can. You've kept us safe. Whatever happens, we'll face it together."

He kissed her lips. "Sorry, I've been such an ass. I'm even sorrier that I have to leave you now."

Josie stared at him, aghast. "What? What are you going to do?" She'd finally gotten him back; she didn't want to lose him again.

"I have to do what I can. The town is defenseless, and I told them I'd protect them. They're counting on me."

Josie knew he was right. A tear slipped down her cheek. Bane brushed it away, then kissed her again.

He rubbed Markley under his chin. "Take care of Mommy."

And then he was gone.

Josie watched him go through the door, leap down the steps, and stride toward his ship. She had never loved him more.

He paused and turned his gaze to the sky. Josie put Markley down and stepped out onto the porch.

Bane suddenly yelled, "Oh, yeah!" and raised his fist in the air.

Josie looked up, wondering what had him all excited. In a daze, she came down the few steps and moved toward him. The sky still buzzed with several small, black alien ships. But two other ships, not quite as large as the invader but many times deadlier in appearance, now flanked the huge UFO. Dozens of silver and reddish-colored ships barreled out of the new arrivals like bees from a hive. The colorful, little ships began firing upon the black ships, and at the same time, the pair of UFOs fired at the larger, menacing ship. For several minutes an air battle took place. And then, with an enormous explosion, the invader ship succumbed.

"What's happening?" Josie cried as flaming pieces of metal rained down to the ground.

Bane pulled her into his arms and twirled her around in a circle. He actually smiled. "We've got back-up. They've come—the Acacians!"

EPILOGUE

Josie sat on the deck of the cabin and stared out at the calm surface of the water. Behind her, she could hear Markley's steady purr as he sat in the window.

It'd been two months since the timely arrival of the Acacians, and Earth's safety had been secured. The Acacians had swarmed the skies and annihilated the enemy. They'd only remained long enough to ensure the human race that help was ever close. And to have faith in the Sentinels, they had entrusted here so long ago.

Sadly, most of the large cities had been destroyed, but thanks to the Sentinels, the small towns thrived and now spilled over with refugees who had barely escaped with their lives.

The townspeople of Albion had worked together to erect new dwellings to house their bulging population. Josie and Bane had become permanent residents and could often be seen lending a hand in town.

Many in town had hung their heads in shame and begged Bane's forgiveness. Surprisingly, he had humbly accepted their apologies and immediately begun overseeing construction in the town. Josie had been amazed at the change in him. No longer did he wear the mask of a reluctant hero. Every day she saw more and more of the man he'd once been resurfacing.

Recently he'd confessed to her the internal struggle he'd faced. How he'd battled what he perceived as his weaker self in order to complete his mission. Startlingly at the height of the madness, it'd been that calmer part of him that had reared up, overcoming the cold shell of the Sentinel and exerting control. Over time more and more instances of old Bane pushed through until, finally, the Sentinel had been forced back into slumber. Josie hoped and prayed to never see that part of him again.

The screen door banged, and Josie turned to

see Bane with two glasses of lemonade. "You read my mind," she said, reaching for the glass.

Instead of sitting down beside her, he leaned against the railing. "Tired?"

"Not so much. Thanks for letting me sleep in so late."

He smiled. "You needed it."

Josie put her hand on her belly, and they smiled at each other conspiratorially.

"I think you should slow down and not work so hard. Things are moving along smoothly in town. The new buildings should be habitable before the snow flies," Bane said.

She sighed. "I think you're right. Lately, all I want to do is sleep." How strange to know that the child she carried would be an only son, just as his lineage dictated.

Bane set down his glass and reached for her hand. "You don't have to worry about them coming back. We did some major damage and substantial upgrading in the security department. Our son won't have to go through this. At least not with the Cadeyrns."

She frowned. "But there are other threats out

there."

"If he's forced to face them, he will be fine. He's never alone. He has us and Gannon watching over him."

"Do you ever want to go there? To Gannon?"

He shrugged. "No. This is my home."

She smiled. "I'm glad. I don't want you to ever leave me again."

"Speaking of which…." He reached out to take her glass and set it down next to his. He pulled her to her feet.

"What're you doing?"

He knelt down on one knee and reached into his pocket.

Josie swallowed hard. "Bane?"

He held up the ring she'd hidden in the dresser. "I love you, Jose, with all my heart. Thank you for standing by my side and helping me save the town. Will you do me the honor of becoming my bride?"

Josie nodded, and her hand shook while Bane slipped the ring on her finger. "I found it on the floor in our apartment the night we were forced to leave."

He frowned. "I was going to propose to you that night."

"I kind of figured."

He kissed the back of her hand and stood up. "And you've had it all this time."

She nodded.

"You must have thought I was such a bastard."

"Maybe just a little," she admitted.

He chuckled over the face she made. "I'm happy you kept it. I'm even happier I found it. Where'd you stash all my underwear, by the way?"

"Second drawer."

He laid his hand over her belly and gently kissed her lips. "I love you so much. Everything will be okay now, I promise."

Josie felt a tear slip down her cheek as he pulled her into his arms. Who knew what the future held? She did know with Bane by her side, she could face anything. All they could do now was hope the world they rebuilt for their child would be one filled with peace.

Juliet is an award-winning author of several best-selling novels and short stories. She lives in Ontario with her husband, cat and dog. You can check out Juliet's website to see what she's been up to.
http://JulietCardinWebsite.Yolasite.com